Emily Sparkes

and the Backstage BLUNDER

by Ruth Fitzgerald

LITTLE, BROWN BOOKS FOR YOUNG READERS
www.lbkids.co.uk

LITTLE, BROWN BOOKS FOR YOUNG READERS

First published in Great Britain in 2016 by Hodder and Stoughton

1 3 5 7 9 10 8 6 4 2

Text copyright © 2016 by Ruth Fitzgerald
Illustrations copyright © 2016 by Allison Cole

The moral rights of the author and illustrator have been asserted.

*All characters and events in this publication other than those
clearly used in the public domain, are fictitious and any resemblance
to real persons, living or dead, is purely coincidental.*

A CIP catalogue record for this book
is available from the British Library.

ISBN 978-0-34900-188-3

Typeset in Minion by M Rules
Printed and bound in Great Britain by
Clays Ltd, St Ives plc

The paper and board used in this book are made from
wood from responsible sources.

MIX
Paper from
responsible sources
FSC® C104740

Little, Brown Books for Young Readers
An imprint of Hachette Children's Group
Part of Hodder and Stoughton
Carmelite House
50 Victoria Embankment
London EC4Y 0DZ

An Hachette UK Company
www.hachette.co.uk

www.hachettechildrens.co.uk

"I have read the first Emily Sparkes book and really
LOVE it … it's lots of fun and a really cool read!"
Cathy Cassidy, bestselling author of
The Chocolate Box Girls series

"Utterly hilarious and utterly relatable,
Ruth Fitzgerald just gets all of the awful problems
associated with being eleven years old. Everything in
Emily Sparkes's life is a crisis, and each crisis is funnier
than the last. Bring on the next book!"
Robin Stevens, author of *Murder Most Unladylike*

"I laughed and laughed at
Emily Sparkes and the Friendship Fiasco!
She's like a younger Georgia Nicolson."
Susie Day, author of *Pea's Book of Best Friends*

"Lots to appeal to fans of Cathy Cassidy and *Dork Diaries*
in this funny new series." *Bookseller*

"Once you start reading this book you won't be
able to put it down. It's true to life and very funny.
Emily Sparkes is everyone's dream best friend!" Alice, 12

"I thought this was side-splittingly funny
and very realistic. Emily Sparkes is someone
I'd want to be friends with!" Sterrett, 10

"Emily Sparkes is my new favourite character.
She made me laugh a lot!" Piper, 11

"Emily Sparkes is amazingly funny." Maddie, 12

For m 700042159087 d.co.uk

By Ruth Fitzgerald

Emily Sparkes and the Friendship Fiasco

Emily Sparkes and the Competition Calamity

Emily Sparkes and the Disco Disaster

Emily Sparkes and the Backstage Blunder

CONTENTS

To Rosie. Front cover next!

CHAPTER 1

{ Act One, Scene One }

Sunday evening

Mostly Bs

You were born for the stage! You are confident and energetic. You love to act and like nothing more than to have an audience. You can sometimes be a bit of a drama

queen, however. Make sure you show your star quality and you'll always be centre stage.

I think these quiz things are rubbish.

Drama queen? When do I have time to be a drama queen? I am too busy dealing with the total stress of coping with my hopeless parents, mad gran, weird neighbours and complicated friends. And I am definitely not confident and energetic. My parents have ruined my confidence by their embarrassing school volunteering activities (in case you don't know, my mum dug up the school field and planted beans and my dad wore tight trousers and tried to be the school disco DJ). Also, I have less energy than a zombie slug and I am virtually dead from malnutrition because my mum never cooks a proper dinner as she is apparently too busy looking after my new baby sister. And I definitely don't want an audience – that would mean that loads more people would get to know about all this stuff.

This was supposed to be a fun homework to get us thinking about what sort of job we'd like. Our head teacher, Mr Meakin, is homework mad. We have homework every night and my teacher, Mrs Lovetofts, is basically always pulling her hair out trying to find something new for us to do. It's amazing she's not completely bald by now. I wouldn't be surprised if she'd found this quiz in the back of a magazine at the dentist's or something, which is not really the best place to find educational materials. Still, as homeworks go I suppose it's a lot better than a page of fractions.

Mostly As means you want to be a doctor; mostly Bs, an actor; mostly Cs, a sportsperson and mostly Ds, a teacher. I would really like to be a camel whisperer, crossing the deserts and helping out people with awkward dromedaries. (I know that sounds like something you should

seek medical advice about, but it's just a posh word for camel. I've been studying.) But camel whisperer is not one of the quiz options.

To be fair, perhaps I didn't answer the questions very well. That's the trouble with this sort of quiz. You can't help trying to work out what they want you to say, rather than what you really think. Like it says:

Your mum takes you shopping to the mall but insists on wearing her embarrassing woolly bobble hat. Do you:

A. Explain that it's not healthy to have a hot head.

B. Buy a similar hat and have a crazy, girly giggle together when everyone stares at you.

C. Run away.

D. Refuse to continue shopping until she displays more acceptable behaviour.

}

Obviously you would do C. Anyone would, even people who are allergic to athletics. No one would really do B, but it's the sort of answer you're supposed to give to show you've got a fun and positive personality. So that's what I ticked. Anyway this would never actually happen to me, as my mum hates clothes shopping and the last time we went to a shopping mall she had a panic attack because she hadn't seen a tree for two hours.

Actually, we *are* doing an end of term play at school. We have auditions tomorrow, so you never know, perhaps the quiz is right and I'm destined for great things on the stage and the camels of the world will just have to get over their behaviour problems by themselves.

Oh, hang on. My ancient, banana-yellow mobile

is making a sound like a dying frog. That means I've got a message. It used to sort of bleep but it hasn't been the same since I accidentally gave it a swimming lesson in a bowl of leek and lettuce soup (more on soup later). Anyway, it'll only be Chloe (my third-best friend, who's a total pain) because Zuzanna's (my second-best friend, who's a bit of a pain) mum has decided she can't use her mobile after 7 o'clock, in case it interferes with her homework and stops her learning to spell properly.

Hi. Wossup?

(I think Zuzanna's mum might have a point.)

Doing homework.

Auditions tomoz.

Who is Tomos?

For goodness' sake Emily. Tomoz. It means TOMORROW.

Oh. Sorry. You could have just said that.

It's supposed to make it quick – although it's not really working here is it?

Sorry. Yes auditions – Tomosoz.

TOMOZ. Are u going for a part?

Yes. Of course.

Really???!!!

What do you mean?

Oh. Nothing. C u tomozoz then. I mean tomos.
Oh, never mind.

I know what she means. I will try my best, but I bet I get chosen to be something totally rubbish. The thing about school plays is that they never have enough parts so the main roles always go to the people who talk the loudest or whose mums are good at making costumes. Then the teachers just make up pointless parts for everyone else. I have been in four school plays. So far I have been: a duck; a shining star (that was just a star but they added the "shining" bit to make it sound more interesting); a "person in the crowd" (basically "a person" – no acting required) and a Roman soldier (there was a whole battalion of us, the teachers must have been really pleased when they came up with that idea). I have never had a speaking part, unless you count "Quack."

At least that's homework finished for tonight. I

have been doing it on the kitchen table (obviously not actually on the table, I put some paper in between) which wasn't very good planning as Mum has just come in to make the dinner. Mum can't stand seeing people doing nothing. If she finds a stray person in the kitchen she'll stick a potato peeler in their hand before they even realise they weren't making themselves useful.

"Hello, love," Mum says. "Finished your homework?" I see her eyes flick towards the dishwasher which probably needs emptying, or filling, or polishing or something.

"Err ... noooooo. No, I've got loads left to do. Phew, they don't half pile it on. Everyone's complaining they've got no time left in the evening for emptying potatoes or peeling dishwashers or anything. And it's all got to be in ... by tomoz."

Mum looks
a bit confused
so I decide to take
the chance and change
the subject quickly. "What's for
dinner?"

If you know about my family, at this point you will be saying to yourself "pasta bake", because until recently that was all my mum cooked, but things have changed. She has moved on to another page of *Fabulous Frugal Food* and now all she cooks is—

"Soup." Mum smiles as if it is something new and exciting and not the same thing we have had every night for the last week.

"We have had quite a lot of soup lately, Mum," I say.

 "Yes, but that's the beauty of soup, you can have endless varieties," Mum says.

"So what sort is it tonight then?" I say, not really wanting to know the answer.

Mum opens the fridge and peers in warily, as if something might jump out of it. "Tonight we are having ..." She pulls out a bag of carrots and dumps them in the middle of the table. "Carrot soup."

"Just carrot? Basically carrot and carrot soup?"

Mum sighs. "No, no – carrot and ..." She closes the fridge and opens the cupboard. "Sardine!" she says triumphantly.

"Carrot and sardine? That is not an actual soup, is it?"

"Well ..." Mum says, delving into the back of the cupboard. "How about carrot and sliced peaches? Sounds quite exotic."

"No. Do we have to have carrot anything?"

"The carrots need using up – we can't just throw them away."

"Why not? I won't tell anybody."

"Because it's wasteful, Emily," Mum says. "The good cook adapts to what's available in her kitchen."

I don't like to remind her that she is not a good cook, in fact she is not even a "you'll just about do" cook. She shouldn't really be called a cook at all, more of an experimental scientist.

"Carrot and marmalade?" she says.

I stuff my homework into my school bag quickly in case it also ends up in the soup, although it might improve it. Also, I cannot think of anything to say which is not going to get me into trouble but luckily my baby sister, Clover, starts crying in the other room so I have a good excuse to escape.

Clover is lying on her back on her baby rug thing, in the living room. She is not really crying much, it's more of an "I'm bored" grizzle. It's not really surprising that she's bored. All she can do at the moment is lie on her back and look at the ceiling and, once you've counted the spider webs, there's probably not much else to think about. I sit down beside her to cheer her up with a chat.

"Did you know, Clover, that it's nearly Christmas? As it's your first ever Christmas I'd better explain how it works."

"Ehhhhhhh!" Clover says. She has been saying this a lot lately. I'm sure she's trying to say "Emily", but nobody else seems to think so. Dad says a baby's first words are always "Dada", so Mum and I will just have to wait our turn.

"You have to decide what presents you'd like and make a list – I did mine in September – then you really hope that, between Father Christmas,

13

Mum, Dad, Gran and all the random aunties and uncles, at least one person manages to get you something that you want. But mostly you get loads of stuff which was never on your list in the first place, like weird bubble bath that makes your skin itchy, cheap chocolate shapes that taste like soap and lots of pairs of fluffy socks. Last year I got some fluffy socks in a tin shaped like a Christmas tree – I still don't really understand why someone thought that was a good idea. Then, after all the presents, everyone has a massive Christmas dinner and Mum gets stressed about sprouts. Then there's a horrible pudding with disgusting wine stuff poured over the top that is supposed

to catch fire but never does, so Mum gets more stressed. Oh, and there are these things called Christmas crackers and they make a loud bang and you have to wear a funny hat. It's all for Baby Jesus's birthday."

I am not sure I've made Christmas sound very much fun, but at least Clover has stopped crying. In fact, now that I come to think about it, Christmas is actually very stressful.

Things to worry about at Christmas
    getting a rubbish part in the school play (very likely)
        getting rubbish presents (quite likely)
        Forgetting someone when you write your class Christmas cards (not very likely because I triple-ish check twelve times and I'm going to write three cards for Zuzanna and Chloe just in case)

Trying to open a card from gross-Out gavin without actually touching the bit of the envelope he licked

Being made to eat a sprout
Being made to eat two sprouts!

Now I have got myself into a state of total worrisome-ness. I need to see if Bella's online. Bella is my first-best friend, and she is not at all a pain. Unfortunately, she moved to Wales in the summer to look after goats. Her best goat is called Clover. (Mum and Dad accidentally named my baby sister after her. I haven't told them because they might decide to call the baby something else, and it took them most of the autumn to come up with that.) Anyway, she is very good at sorting out worries (Bella, not the goat).

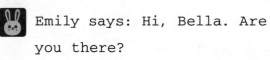 

Emily says: Hi, Bella. Are you there?

Bella says: Yes. You OK?

Emily says: I'm worrying about Christmas.

Bella says: You are the world's greatest worrier. This will cheer you up. Guess what?

Emily says: What?

Bella says: We are coming up in a couple of weeks, just for one night. Mum has to sort some paperwork out and we're staying with Auntie Penny.

Emily says: Oh, wow! That's so cool. You can come round and see my new room.

17

Bella says: I probably won't recognise you any more!

Emily says: You probably have a Welsh accent!

Bella says: Everyone here thinks I speak posh. I think that's why they gave me a good part in the play. We're doing *The Lion, the Witch and the Wardrobe* and I'm going to be Lucy.

Emily says: That's cool.

Bella says: I know. It's the best part really – I've got so much to learn. Emily is really good at acting. She does Stage Club at the weekends. She's giving me loads of help.

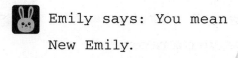 Emily says: You mean New Emily.

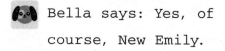 Bella says: Yes, of course, New Emily.

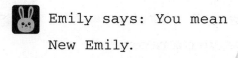 Emily says: We have auditions tomoz. I hope I get a good part, too.

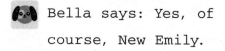 Bella says: Who's Tomos?

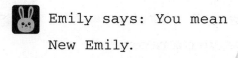 Emily says: Never mind.

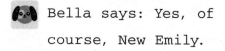 Bella says: New Emily says you've got to speak up really loudly and wave your arms about a bit so they know you're not shy.

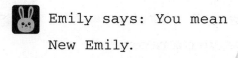 Emily says: Oh. OK.

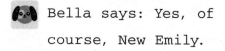 Bella says: And New Emily says you have to look directly at

your audience
and make sure you
stand up straight.

Emily says: I'm going to
really go for it. I need
to get a decent part
for once.

Bella says: Ha ha!
You always get rubbish
parts. Remember when you
were a duck? "Quaaaack"!

Emily says: Well, I am not
willing to be a duck any more!
And I'm so excited about you
coming back!

Bella says: Me too. Got to
go. Emily's coming over to
practise our lines.

Emily says: You mean New Emily.

Bella doesn't answer. She must have gone already.

CHAPTER 2

Be Careful What You Fish For ...

Monday morning

This morning, as usual, I am walking to school with Lena, my next door neighbour. She's in Year Five and hasn't been at our school long. Lena likes black clothes and eyeliner and wandering about looking moody. At her last school she got picked on because of the way she looks but she's really nice once you get used to her. Oh, yes, and her dad's a sort of rock star person.

"We're doing auditions for the Year Six play today," I say. "Are your class doing a play?"

"No, we're just having a singing concert. Mrs Ahmed says she can't be doing with any more drama this term. She's been very nervy since Harry Passmore swung on the stage curtains and pulled them down on top of her, in that assembly about circus performers. It's a pity, because I love school plays."

"I wouldn't have thought acting would be your thing."

"No, not acting – I mean making scenery, doing the sound and lighting and all that backstage stuff. I sometimes help my dad out when he does concerts."

"I'm really hoping to get a good part this time," I say, as we meet Zuzanna outside her house.

24

"Really, Emily?" Zuzanna says. "You're going to audition for a part?"

awesome

"Don't you start," I say. "Why does everyone think I can't act?"

"Maybe because of the time you were a Roman soldier and you dropped your shield off the stage and it hit Alfie's grandad on the head?"

"That was because Joshua bumped into me—"

"Or the time you were a shining star and you poked Mina Begum in the eye with one of your pointy star bits and she had to do the rest of the play with one eye closed?"

"She was fine – she was just putting it on."

"Or the time—"

"OK, OK. I get it, but I've just had a bit of bad luck with plays. From now on my luck is going to change, you'll see."

At school, Mrs Lovetofts gets everyone sitting down to make an announcement about the play. Chloe is trying to tell me about the new coat she's getting, which is, apparently, the most fashionable thing in the entire world of fashionable-ness, but I am mostly ignoring her and listening very hard to Mrs Lovetofts. I really want to get a good part and show Bella that I'm just as good as New Emily, even if I don't go to a posh Stage Club.

Mrs Lovetofts says, "This year I have written another play especially for our class. It's an exciting mystery set in Tudor times. It is called *The Lost Crown*." She pauses for us to say "Ooh," but not many people do – Mrs Lovetofts' plays don't usually inspire a lot of "oohing". (Actually, they should probably inspire a bit of booing, but the parents are always too polite.) And, unfortunately, the pause is longer than Alfie and Gavin's attention span and we have to waste another three minutes while Mrs Lovetofts explains that the proper place for an earwax-eating challenge is in the playground and not the classroom.

"So, back to the play," Mrs Lovetofts says. "You will all be thrilled to know that our talented music specialist, Mrs Harris, has written a song for us to sing at the end!" She claps her hands with excitement. I think calling Mrs Harris "a music specialist" is going a bit far – basically she is the only teacher who can play the piano, and when I say "play" I really mean "hit".

"So we will all need to be warming up our vocal chords," she continues. "La la la la la la la."

A song. Oh, dear. Singing is totally not my thing. I mean, I like singing, it's just that other people don't seem to like listening to me. When we did "Bringing in the Sheaves" at the Harvest Festival, Chloe said I had a very good voice for Harvest because I sounded like a tractor.

"Stage, song, spotlights! What more is there to life?" Mrs Lovetofts hugs her chest and looks dreamily up at the ceiling as if she is hoping a spotlight will shine on her.

"Cake? Chocolate? *Hollyoaks*?" says Amy-Lee Langer, but Mrs Lovetofts ignores her, or maybe she's just too caught up in her theatre dreams. Fortunately, Alfie Balfour does a loud burp and that seems to bring her back down to earth.

Chloe shoots her hand in the air. "How many starring roles are there, Miss?"

"Well, of course every part is important. A play is all about working together," smiles Mrs Lovetofts.

"Yes but how many *properly* important parts?"

"If you mean speaking parts, there's the queen, the witch, the innkeeper and his wife. But as I said, Chloe, no one part

28

is more important than any other – everyone will get a part of some sort. We need lots of townsfolk to do country dancing between scenes."

I sigh. That'll be me. A country-dancing villager. I really hate country dancing.

"At my last school we had acting lessons with Emma Watson," Chloe says. "I was a natural."

"Yeah, a natural show-off," Amy-Lee Langer says.

"Yeah," Yeah-Yeah Yasmin agrees.

"At least I have something to show off about," Chloe says.

"If your old school is so good why don't you go back there?" Amy-Lee says.

"Yeah," Yeah-Yeah Yasmin says.

"Because I feel it's my mission to help educate the less intelligent," Chloe says.

Amy-Lee jumps to her feet, although she seems a bit unsure what to do next.

"Now then ladies," says Mrs Lovetofts, "let's all try to be friends." Which is a bit like asking the Daleks and Doctor Who to play nicely.

"Is there a narrator?" Zuzanna asks. "I so love reading."

"Yes, there's a narrator, too," Mrs Lovetofts says and I see Zuzanna cross her fingers.

"Are there any ducks?" I ask.

"Ducks?" says Mrs Lovetofts. "Err, no. No ducks."

Phew. At least that's one thing less to worry about.

"Anyway," Mrs Lovetofts continues, "I will be holding auditions in the hall at lunchtime to allocate roles. So pop along and try your luck!"

I know I should think positively but it's not easy. People like Chloe and Zuzanna always get the good parts – I need something to make me stand out from the crowd. I've got to show Bella that I can get a good part too. What I need is some Emily Sparkes creativityness to get Mrs Lovetofts to notice my special acting talents.

I flick Wavey Cat's paw. Wavey Cat is my Japanese good luck cat – Bella bought him for me before she left. I often bring him to school and sit him on my table. He never seems to bring good luck in the way you want but he's my best hope at the moment. "I need Mrs Lovetofts to pick me for a good part in the play," I say. Well, I don't actually "say", because that would be embarrassing. I just think it – loudly.

Wavey Cat waves his little paw and Mrs Lovetofts says, "Right then, that's enough chatter about the play. Time to get on with some work."

"Yeah, well done, Wavey Cat," I mutter. "Really helpful, as usual."

"Babette, can you collect up the homework, please?" Mrs Lovetofts says.

I reach into my bag to get my homework folder out and then I have an idea. Maybe Wavey Cat has given me a bit of creativityness after all.

Babette wanders around the class collecting up the folders. "Homework, please," she says when she gets to our table. Chloe and Zuzanna hand over their folders but I keep scrabbling around in my school bag. "It's in here somewhere," I say to Babette, who is waiting patiently.

"Isn't that it?" she says, pointing to a red folder sticking out of my bag.

"No – no, that's just another folder that looks like it," I say, shoving the red folder down.

"But it says 'Homework' on it," Babette says.

"No ... no, that's a mistake. It actually says 'Literacy' but I ... err ... spelled it wrong. Probably spending too much time on my mobile." I laugh, quickly closing my bag. "Look, don't

worry. You collect
the rest and I'll bring
mine up in a minute, when I find it."

Babette pulls a face and stomps off to collect the rest of the homework folders, which she drops in a pile on Mrs Lovetofts' desk.

"Found it," I say, and pull my homework folder out of my bag.

Babette spins round to look. "But that's the one I just saw," she says, crossly.

"Oh, yes, silly me," I say.

Babette snatches it out of my hand and slaps my folder right on the top of the pile in front of Mrs Lovetofts.

Success! Mrs Lovetofts always marks the first few homework folders at breaktime. She is bound to see mine first and then she will read my homework quiz and realise that I am born to be an actor. Good job I cheated on the answers and double good job there was no camel whisperer option.

At lunchtime Chloe and Zuzanna are all excited about the auditions.

"I am so looking forward to being the queen," Chloe says, nibbling regally at her peanut butter sandwich.

"You might not get it, Chloe," Zuzanna says.

"I will," Chloe says. "We did *Matilda* at Mag Hall. Emma cast me in the lead, of course. She was going to get me into the West End musical but, to be honest, I was too busy."

Zuzanna rolls her eyes at me. "I really want to be the narrator," she says. "I mean, like, more than anything."

"You're bound to get it, Zuzanna," I say, "you are the best reader in the school."

"Thanks," Zuzanna says, "and you must be really pleased there're no quacking parts."

Actually, I'm feeling very hopeful. At breaktime I hung around just long enough in class to see Mrs Lovetofts start marking my homework. She was definitely smiling. She must have some confidence in me now.

"Come on," Chloe says, "let's go and line up. We want Mrs Lovetofts to see how enthusiastic we are. And Emily, be careful to walk, not waddle," she

 adds. "Just in case they find a duck part for you after all." She strolls off in a sort of slow, royal-ish way.

There is a bit of a queue outside the hall already and we join the end. Everyone seems excited. I am trying not to get too nervous.

"Auditions, this way," says Mrs Lovetofts, bustling past.

We all file into the hall behind her.

"Right, quieten down everyone," she says.

"This is all very exciting," I say loudly, to show I can project my voice.

"Yes, Emily," she says. "But there's no need to shout. Perhaps you're getting a little over-enthusiastic."

"I can't help it. I just love the stage," I say in what I hope sounds like an actor-ish voice, and I wave my arms around a bit, like New Emily suggested.

"Ouch," snaps Zuzanna as I accidentally knock her glasses sideways. "Be careful, Emily. What are you doing? You look like a windmill."

"Sorry," I say. Mrs Lovetofts doesn't seem to have noticed anyway, she is talking to Mrs Harris, who has just come in.

Then I hear a strange noise. I turn around to see Chloe standing very straight with her hands clasped in front of her. She has her eyes closed and is sort of snorting through her nose.

"Are you all right, Chloe?" says Zuzanna. "You sound a bit wheezy."

"Indeed," Chloe says in a slow, deep voice. "We are just doing our breathing exercises."

"We?" Zuzanna says, looking around. "Who's we?"

Chloe sighs and opens one eye. "It's the *royal* we," she says. "It's what Queen Elizabeth says when she's talking about herself."

"Does she?" I say. "I've never heard her say that."

"Precisely how many times have you spoken with the Queen, Emily?" Chloe snaps.

"Well, err ... "

"Exactly. Now please be quiet. I am trying to get into character."

I am not sure what character she is getting into. Really, she mostly reminds me of Darth Vader – if he was a lot shorter and had blonde hair and a school sweatshirt.

Mrs Lovetofts claps her hands together and says, "Thank you, everyone, for coming along.

If you could line up at the side of the room, Mrs Harris will be starting the auditions in a couple of minutes."

Mrs Harris?

"But Miss, aren't you doing the auditions?" I ask, feeling slightly panicky.

"I'm afraid not. Mr Meakin has just called me to an urgent meeting – I expect it's about overuse of stationery supplies again," she says, looking worried. "I'm sure you'll all be marvellous, though," she continues, brightening. "And, after all, Mrs Harris is my production assistant." Mrs Harris scowls at this but Mrs Lovetofts responds with her usual beaming smile. "I look forward to finding out who has got which part later on," she says and bustles out again.

Disaster! Mrs Harris doesn't like me at all. All because once, *just once*, my school-dinner fish finger ended up in her mug of tea. It totally wasn't my fault. If Other Emily B.

hadn't put her violin case where
it wasn't supposed to be I wouldn't
have tripped over it, and my plate
wouldn't have flown off the lunch tray and
my fish finger wouldn't have launched into the
air and sailed into Mrs Harris's mug. But she was
really cross – she said I must have thrown it on
purpose.

Really, if I could throw a fish finger that well I'd
be in the seafood Olympics. If she really thought
I'd done it deliberately I think she should have
given me a sports achievement house point, not a
lunchtime detention.

Anyway, that was weeks ago but she still doesn't
seem to have forgiven me. She said she can no
longer enjoy a cup of tea without tasting cod. She
has definitely just given me a hard stare. I am
starting to feel very nervous.

We have to stand on a table in front of Mrs
Harris to audition. Apparently the stage is "off

limits" at the moment due to health and safety concerns about the curtains. I think there should be more health and safety concerns about having to stand on a table but that doesn't seem to have occurred to Mrs Harris. She is sitting on a chair behind a desk and has made herself a sign which says "Casting Director". I knew she didn't like being called "Production Assistant".

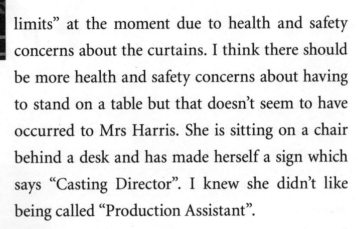

"When I call your name, go and stand on the table and repeat the line, 'Oh dear, I feel very strange. I think the witch has put a spell on me!' And no messing about in the queue," she snaps, scowling at Gross-Out and Alfie who look very surprised as they haven't even started messing about yet – they are still at the planning stage.

Mrs Harris coughs loudly and shouts, "Action!" She is being totally bossy – I think the power has gone to her head.

Zuzanna is up first. She has to have a bit of a

hand to get up on the table but once she's up there she does look very confident. She says in a very clear and calm voice, "The queen was feeling very strange, and to make matters worse she thought it was entirely possible that the witch had put a spell on her."

"Zuzanna," says Mrs Harris with a sigh, "this is an audition. You are supposed to act, not tell us a story."

"I don't really want to act," Zuzanna says. "I want to be the narrator."

"Next!" says Mrs Harris and scribbles something on the pad in front of her.

After Zuzanna it is Chloe's turn. She climbs up on the table and closes her eyes. She stands still for a moment, then she starts taking noisy deep breaths again.

"Do you need to go to the sick room, Chloe?" asks Mrs Harris.

"I'm just building up to my role," says

Chloe. "Emma Watson always does this before a performance."

"Well do you think you could build a little more quickly? I already have a headache," Mrs Harris says, scowling even more.

Suddenly, Chloe puts her hands up to her neck and starts scrabbling at it wildly, then she gasps and falls to her knees.

I am just thinking someone should call an ambulance when she wails, "Oh! Oh! I feel so strange. I think the witch has put a spell on me!"

"Next," says Mrs Harris, scribbling on her list.

"But I haven't started crying yet," Chloe says and makes a strange blubbing noise.

"NEXT!"

Really, I don't know what has got into Mrs Harris, she's usually a quiet sort of teacher. Well, apart from when she's got fish in her tea.

Chloe makes a loud, huffy noise and

climbs down from the table in a very un-royal sort of way. "It's so difficult working with amateurs," she mutters.

Unfortunately, next is me. I am feeling very nervous now. Not only does Mrs Harris not like me and not know anything about my newly discovered acting skills but she is also getting in a very bad mood. I'm sure the next person to upset her will get sent to Mr Meakin. Still, I have to be brave. I am determined to have a good part this time. It's my last chance. I am leaving Juniper Road Primary next summer and that will be it for my junior acting career. I do not want to be forever remembered as the girl who said, "Quack."

I climb up on the table and take a deep breath. I decide not to wave my arms about because, even though New Emily might be good at acting, I'll bet she never had to do it standing on a wobbly table in front of a grouchy teacher. But when I look at Mrs Harris I can't stop thinking about the tea incident and it is very difficult to remember everything I am supposed to do. I am concentrating so hard on trying to project my voice and stand up straight and look at the audience and also not fall off the table, that when it's time to speak I say, really loudly, "Oh dear, I feel very strange. I think the fish has put a smell on me!"

I clap my hand over my mouth. Why did I say that? Disaster!

Everyone in the room bursts out laughing. Well, everyone except Mrs Harris.

Gross-Out Gavin shouts, "Oh, is that smell you, Emily? I thought it was coming from Mrs Harris's mug!"

Everyone laughs even more. I feel my cheeks burning red.

"NEXT!" yells Mrs Harris. She looks down at her piece of paper and scribbles a note. I try to get down from the table but I can't seem to move. I have sort of got frozen with nerves. I have got table fright!

"Get down, Emily," Mrs Harris growls.

"I . . . I'm stuck," I stammer.

Mrs Harris narrows her eyes. "Will someone, anyone, please help Emily get down from the table, as she appears to have lost the use of her legs."

Zuzanna hurries over and puts her hand up to help me down. "Really, Emily," she whispers, "you need to be more professional if you want to get a part."

Then I have to walk back through the hall past a whole line of giggling children and Gavin and Alfie who both hold their noses and say, "Phoarrrr!" and "Pooh!" and "What's that fishy stink?"

I just know nothing like this ever happens to New Emily.

CHAPTER 3

Who's Queen?

Still Monday

I have to sit in the book corner for the rest of lunchtime just to recover. It's better than going out to play anyway, because Chloe and Zuzanna are practising their bows and curtain calls and I don't think there's much point me joining in now. I have totally ruined my chances of getting a part. I am a disastrous drama drop-out.

47

After lunch Mrs Lovetofts seems very excited. "Hurry up and settle down, Year Six," she says. "I'm dying to tell you the exciting news," and she does a little giggle.

Chloe smiles smugly. "She's going to announce my role," she says. "She's probably found out about my Oscar nomination. I don't usually mention it."

Mrs Lovetofts takes a deep breath and says, "Every year, the Shoestring Theatre, our very own theatre in the town centre, chooses a couple of local schools to perform a play in their Christmas Gala. This year I entered *The Lost Crown*. Of course, I never thought it would get anywhere ... I mean, I'm just an amateur playwright. Not Shakespeare or anything." She stops and does another little giggle.

"I hope there's a point to this story," mutters Chloe. "It's taken up a whole minute of my life already."

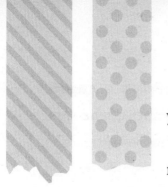

"The thing is – well. This year ... we have been chosen!"

Everyone gasps, although I'm not sure if it's because they're excited or surprised – after all, Mrs Lovetofts' school plays have never been very good before.

"The amazing thing is," she continues, "we will now get to rehearse and perform the play at a real, live, proper theatre, with a real stage and lighting and everything."

There are more gasps from the class. This time they are definitely due to everyone being excited.

"Imagine," Zuzanna sighs, "being in a real theatre production. Oh, I so want to be the narrator!"

"Of course, at Mag Hall we had a theatre in the grounds," Chloe says, "so it's nothing new for me, but it will be nice for everyone else to see my acting talents properly displayed."

"You don't know if you've got a good part yet," Amy-Lee says. "Maybe you'll end up being a dancing villager."

"Yeah," Yeah-Yeah Yasmin says.

"That idea is so stupid it could only have come from you," Chloe says. "Or Yasmin ... or Gross-Out ... or Alfie ... or—"

"Tomorrow morning," Mrs Lovetofts says loudly, to distract everyone before there's a class fight, "we'll walk down to the theatre to take a look at where we'll be performing the play. We will have to practise very hard though, as we only get to use the theatre for a week before the performance. But I know we can do it, it's going to be such fun!" She claps her hands together and does a little twirl around, which is quite dangerous, given how close she is standing to the "Fruits of Autumn" display (although it's about time that came down anyway).

"And," she continues, "as if that wasn't enough, this afternoon we are going to start a new mini-topic!" Strangely this doesn't seem to cause quite as much of a thrill as the theatre news. "Now then, as it's nearly Christmas I thought we'd do a special set of lessons related to that theme."

"Oooh," Gracie says. "Are we going to make decorations?"

"Or bake mince pies?" Joshua says.

"Or get presents?" Amy-Lee says.

"No, no," Mrs Lovetofts says. "As you probably know, Father Christmas is said to live in Lapland, which, of course, is part of Finland. So . . . I thought we'd do a special mini-topic on this fascinating part of Europe. The Nordic countries."

School can be very disappointing at times.

Mrs Lovetofts tries her best, but Geography is not at all interesting and everyone is too excited about the play to learn to spell "aurora borealis". I am feeling a lot better, too. I am trying to be positive. It's still possible that I could get a good part. I mean, I know I messed up the line in the audition but apart from saying the wrong words, turning bright red, upsetting Mrs Harris and getting stuck on the table, it went fine.

Finally, at the end of the day, Mrs Lovetofts hands out the letters with the play parts. "As I said, we're going to the theatre tomorrow morning. Please remember you will be representing the whole school, so proper uniform must be worn. That means no trainers, Alfie, no earring, Joshua, and Gavin, please wear the trousers with the working zip. Girls, please make sure you do not have nail varnish on, and that includes the felt-pen variety," she says, looking right at me.

I stick my hands under the table. They are a bit colourful but that's because I wanted to try out my new pens, and

a picture of a glacier
doesn't call for much Raspberry Red.

"Now, don't forget what I said, everyone – no one part is more important than another," Mrs Lovetofts continues over the sound of the home-time bell. "Having a speaking role doesn't make you more important to the success of the play than someone who doesn't speak."

"Yeah, right," Chloe says. "Only someone completely stupid would believe that."

"It's true," says Gross-Out Gavin, who has already ripped open his envelope and is looking down at his letter. "Non-speaking parts are important, too."

"Thank you for proving my point," Chloe says. "Look. Everyone knows that speaking parts are the most important. How would you know what's going on, otherwise?"

"Not always," Nicole says. "What about mime? No one speaks in a mime show."

"Yes," Babette says. "It's very popular in France."

"Well, they have to mime there because they speak in a foreign language, how would anyone understand them?" Chloe says.

I am still trying to work this out when there is a shriek from behind me and Zuzanna waves her letter in the air. "I'm the narrator! I'm the narrator!" she says and does a little twirl around.

"I'm the innkeeper's wife," Small Emily B. says, beaming around at everyone.

"And I'm the innkeeper!" Alfie says, and Small Emily B.'s smile sort of sinks a bit.

"I'm the witch!" Amy-Lee Langer says. "Heh heh heh! You'd all better watch out. I'll turn you into frogs."

"Yeah," Yasmin says.

"I think the word you're looking for is *ribbit*, Yasmin," Chloe says.

Everyone is chatting excitedly about their parts. I clutch my letter in my hand. I want to open it and I don't want to open it at the same time.

"So come on then. Who's the queen?" Gracie says.

"Well, I don't think there's much doubt about that, is there, dahlinks?" Chloe says, tearing open her envelope.

I turn my back on everyone, take a deep breath and carefully open my letter, too.

I wasn't hoping for much. I mean, you can't go round randomly ranting about fishy smells and expect to get away with it – but when I read my letter it was worse than I could have imagined. I shoved it in the bottom of my bag and ran out of school, just as Chloe was saying, "And yes, you can call me Your Majesty."

It has been stuffed in there all evening and I still don't want to look at it. My mum thinks I'm ill because I didn't want to eat my tea (parsnip and celery soup – you'd have to be ill to *want* to eat it) and sent me upstairs for a lie-down, but the truth is I just don't feel hungry. I keep thinking about standing on the table with everyone laughing at me. My last ever chance to get a good part in a Juniper Road School play and I blew it with a smelling mistake.

I get the letter out with a sigh and flatten it out on my bedside table. Perhaps I read it wrong. If I read it again it might have magically changed to give me a starring role. I flick Wavey Cat's paw and close my eyes. But unfortunately, when I open them it still says the same thing:

Dear parents, carers, etc., etc.
This year's school play will once
 again be a specially written
 production by Mrs Lovetofts,
 entitled The Lost Crown.
Your child has been chosen to play

a rock (number 2)

Costume details will be sent out later this week.
Yours playfully!
Mrs Lovetofts
Drama Co-ordinator/Writer/Producer/
 Director/Costume Designer/Stage
 Manager/Scenery Advisor
Mrs Harris
Assistant

A rock! How can you play a rock? That doesn't
need someone who can act, it just needs someone

who can stand still, which is basically anyone except Alfie Balfour. It must be because I froze – Mrs Harris clearly thought that standing still was my only talent. She obviously doesn't think I can be trusted to say anything. I mean, I wasn't expecting to be given the part of the queen or the witch, but a rock? Not even rock number one. Rock number two, the second most important rock. Even a "townsfolk" would have been better – at least they've got moving parts. If only Mrs Lovetofts had done the auditions, things might have been different. She wouldn't have given up on me just for the sake of a petty pronunciation problem.

So now you see why I am mostly trying to banish it utterly from my mind. I haven't even shown the letter to my mum. She doesn't take much notice of letters from school anyway, but I'm not taking any chances. I know what will happen: Mum will try to make me feel better by saying that being a rock is actually a very difficult part to do well and Mrs Harris must have thought I was up to the challenge, or some other obviously untrue stuff like that. Then my dad will find out and make totally unfunny jokes, like "Stone me, that's a hard part," and say I'm being grumpy when I don't laugh.

And now I am wondering who rock number one is. They must have been chosen to be a rock first. It must be someone who makes an even better rock than me. I don't know if that's a good thing or a bad thing. They may as well give the part to the sock monkey that Mrs Lovetofts keeps on her desk, for all the acting ability it needs.

I don't know what I'm going to say to Bella.

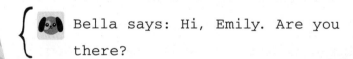 Bella says: Hi, Emily. Are you there?

Emily says: Hi, Bella.

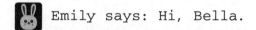 Bella says: Hi. So did you get a part in the school play?

Bella says: Emily, are you there??

Emily says: It's really exciting. We are going to do the play in a real theatre.

Bella says: Wow, that sounds amazing. So which part did you get?

Emily says: Is it still raining there?

Bella says: You got a rubbish part again, didn't you? Didn't you follow New Emily's advice?

Emily says: Yes.

Bella says: And you still got a rubbish part?

I can't tell her. I just can't bring myself to type *rock*.

> Emily says: No I didn't, actually. I got the lead. I am the queen.

> Bella says: Really? Oh, that's amazing! Wait till I tell New Emily her advice worked!

> Emily says: Yeah. She should be really pleased with herself.

I don't know why I did that. I've never lied to Bella before (well, I did once tell her I liked her new school shoes when they actually made her feet look like shiny black Cornish pasties, but that wasn't a bad lie). I am totally fed up with today, it has been all-over rubbish. I'm going to bed.

CHAPTER 4

Rock On

Tuesday morning

This morning I was still fed up. I thought I might get some sympathy so I took a deep breath and told Mum I got the part of a rock. She said, "Oh, good. That should be a nice easy costume. Just grey leggings and a T-shirt."

Typical. She has no thought for how I am feeling, she is just worried about how much work the costume will be. I don't want to stand on stage in grey leggings. To be honest, I don't want to stand on stage at all any more.

 I get outside and it is raining, which makes me feel even more miserable. Luckily, Lena has gone to the dentist's, because I'm in too much of a fed-up mood to talk to her. I have to talk to Zuzanna, though, who is already standing outside her house waiting for me under her NV Boyz umbrella. She is frowning a 3.7 on the frown scale, which is not too bad considering it's raining.

"Emily. You disappeared really quickly yesterday. Which part did you get in the end?"

I think about lying to Zuzanna as well but there's no point because she'd only find out at the first rehearsal. I sigh. "It's just a rubbish part."

"What is it? Come on, it can't be worse than the time you were a duck. Do you remember that? 'Quaaaack!' Ha ha!"

"A rock," I mumble.

"A what?"

"A rock. I'm playing a rock."

Zuzanna sighs. "Oh, dear. That is actually worse than a duck, just. But you can't really expect to get a good part if you can't even get one line right in an audition."

"It was just a mistake. Anyone could have said it. I bet I could be really good at acting if someone would just give me a proper chance."

"Never mind," Zuzanna says. "At least you don't have any lines to learn. Just think how many mistakes you could make if you had to remember a whole play."

When we arrive at school, Chloe is already at our table. "Ah, good morning, peasants," she says.

"Kindly pull out my chair
for me. And you," she
nods in my direction,
"may take the royal coat and hang it
in the cloakroom." She dumps her soggy parka
into my arms and turns back to Zuzanna. "We are
waiting," she says.

"Pull out your chair?" Zuzanna says. "Do it
yourself. Why should I?"

"Because I'm the queen and you're not." Chloe
smiles serenely.

"You are not the queen, Chloe. You just have the
part of the queen in the play."

"You have clearly never heard of method acting,
Zuzanna. Real actors do not just put on an act for
an hour or so, they live and breathe the part. They
actually *become* the character."

"Ith onwy a thcool pway, Chwowe," I say from
behind a mouthful of furry coat hood.

"Only a school play!" says Chloe. "Well it's

no wonder you don't get decent roles with that attitude. What part did you get, anyway?"

I sigh. "A wock."

"A wok?" Chloe says. "Isn't that some sort of frying pan?"

"A *rock*," Zuzanna says. "Emily has got the part of a rock."

"OMG. Sometimes it is so embarrassing being your friend," Chloe says. "Now, hang up the royal parka and make sure you don't crease it, it's new – and totes on trend – so stop chewing my hood." She opens her school bag and pulls out a crumpled up piece of glittery gold card.

"Whaff's that?" I ask.

"It's my royal crown, of course," she says, trying to smooth out the wrinkles. "I made it last night, although it got a bit damp in the

rain." Chloe sits the crumply crown on her head. "There, now I really feel the part," she says.

"You've got glitter on your nose," Zuzanna says.

"Enough of the chit-chat," Chloe says. "If you could hurry along with the chair-pulling-out thing – my royal legs are getting tired."

Zuzanna sighs and pulls out Chloe's chair. Chloe sinks down into it slowly, keeping her back very straight, and folds her hands into her lap. I trudge off to the cloakroom. I think this is going to be a very long day.

"Right, class," Mrs Lovetofts says. "When you have settled down we will take the register and then we can head off to the – oh, I'm so excited! – theatre. Now then, Alfie Balfour?"

"Here, Miss."

"Chloe Clarke?"

"One is totally, royally present," Chloe says.

Mrs Lovetofts looks up. "Sorry? Oh, I see. Very nice Chloe, but no need to get into character quite yet."

"I'm wasted here," Chloe mutters.

"And also, Chloe, beautiful as it may be, that crown is not part of the Juniper Road uniform, is it?"

"But I need it to get into character," Chloe says. "It makes me feel glamorous. Even more than I already am."

"Glamorous?" Gross-Out Gavin says. "More like ridiculous."

"It must be difficult to go through life being so ignorant, Gavin," Chloe says. "No wonder you got the part of a rock."

69

"What?" I am in shock. Even more shock than I was, which was already quite a lot. In fact, I am in rock-shock. "Gross-Out is the other rock?" I say to Chloe.

"Yes. Didn't you know? He's rock number one. Kind of like your partner ... only slightly more important."

I can't believe it. Mrs Harris has cast me in the same role as a boy whose idea of fun is conducting his own Bushtucker Trials with earwigs on the school field. How did she ever think that we could be a double act? My gran is always going on about the state of teacher training in this country and I'm beginning to think she has a point.

Mrs Lovetofts finishes the register and says, "Now I know everyone's going to be on their best behaviour." (No they're not. Some people don't even have a best behaviour. Gross-Out doesn't even have a second-best behaviour, he starts off at about third-best and goes downhill from there.)

"We will be meeting the theatre manager and also the other school who are performing. Now don't forget, class, there's no competition between schools, it's all friendly fun. We are just there to have a lovely experience."

Mrs Lovetofts has a lot to learn about the world.

"It's so thrilling," Zuzanna says, as we troop across the theatre car park. "I came here when I was five to see *Snow White*. I can't believe I'm actually going to be on the same stage as those real actors."

"Side of the stage," Chloe says. "Narrators always stand at the side. I suppose really they should be heard and not seen, don't you think?" She smiles

sweetly. "Of course, I'll be right in the mid—"
Chloe stops chattering with a gasp and I follow
her gaze across the car park to where a shiny white
school minibus has just pulled up. It has the name
of the school on the side but I can't quite see all of
it. Something . . . ALL SCHOOL, with a sort of coat
of arms of a tree in a shield.

"OMG!" Chloe says and runs ahead into the
theatre.

CHAPTER 5

Theatre of Dreams

Still Tuesday morning

"What's up with her?" Zuzanna says.

At that moment the bus pulls forward to reveal the full school name.

MAGNOLIA HALL SCHOOL FOR GIRLS.

"Magnolia Hall? That's Mag Hall, right? Chloe's old school!" I say.

"Is that the other school?" Zuzanna asks.

"Wow. I didn't even think it was real. I kind of thought Chloe made it up."

"But why did Chloe run off? You'd have thought she'd want to say hello."

We go into the theatre and stand in reception. Chloe is nowhere to be seen.

"Look, here they come," Zuzanna says.

A short, tubby man with a yellow scarf strides in from the car park. "Come along, ladies," he says in a loud voice, holding the door open. An assortment of girls in brown school uniforms shuffle into place on the other side of the reception area. None of them look very friendly. I try to avoid making eye contact. Their teacher walks up to Mrs Lovetofts, seizes her hand and shakes it vigorously.

"Vic Garrick, Magnolia Hall Director of Dramatic Arts, actor and playwright."

"Nice to meet you. I'm Mrs Lovetofts, err ... teacher," Mrs Lovetofts says, rubbing her hand.

"Oh yes, of course, I'm also a teacher," he mutters.

"Is this all of your class?" Mrs Lovetofts asks. "Just five?"

Mr Garrick gives a thin smile. "At Magnolia Hall we believe in quality, not quantity," he says. "Let me introduce you. This is Lavender."

"Hi," mutters a tall girl with thin plaits, in a can't be bothered sort of way.

"And Naemah."

Naemah is wearing a brown hijab over her hair. She sort of ducks down into it and mutters, "Hello."

"And Edwina."

The most noticeable thing about Edwina is that she has a very red nose. She doesn't say anything, just blows her red nose loudly.

"And I'm Bianca," says a girl with a blonde bun, stepping forward and smiling broadly. "Nice to meet you all. I'm sure we're going to get along really well." At least one of them seems quite nice.

"You forgot me," says a small voice.

"Oh, so I did," Mr Garrick says, with a sigh. "This is Willow."

"Hello," says a short, chubby girl. "I'm new!"

"Willow has just started with us this week," Mr Garrick says. "She's very ... enthusiastic."

"Oh, yes. I am," Willow says. "I'm going to play the part of the page boy, aren't I?"

"It's not a speaking part," Mr Garrick says, "if you can believe that."

Suddenly there is a squealing, giggling sound from outside and about ten tiny girls burst in through the door, followed by a very harassed looking teacher.

"Oh. And these are our littlees," Mr Garrick says.

"Quiet!" the teacher says and the little girls huddle together and giggle a little less noisily.

"The infant ballet class," he explains, turning back to Mrs Lovetofts. "Very sweet but rather a

handful. And I see you have . . .
a wide range of pupils."

I look at our class. There
is Amy-Lee with her scraggy
skirt glaring at the Mag Hall girls
and probably wondering if they've got any
sweets worth pinching. Next to her, of course, is
Yeah-Yeah Yasmin, chewing gum and staring into
space. I have no idea why Mrs Harris gave them
both a part. They're probably holding her puppy
to ransom or something. Alfie and Gross-Out are
blowing snot bubbles at each other and Joshua is
playing keepy-uppy with a paper cup. In fact, when
you look at them from the outside, pretty much
everyone in our class is a bit weird. Gracie and
Zuzanna are at least looking fairly normal – well,
if you ignore Gracie's coat, which is bright yellow
and has "Horses Are People Too" written across
the back.

Then the theatre manager strolls into the lobby.

She has pink and turquoise stripes in her short blonde hair which makes her seem very arty and interesting. "Hello all," she says, "I'm Elaine. I hope you've all been getting acquainted."

"Hello," Mrs Lovetofts says. "It's so exciting to be here."

Mr Garrick says, "Yes. It must be nice for your school to get to use some proper facilities for a change."

"He's a bit of a show off," Zuzanna whispers. "I don't blame Chloe for leaving that school." She looks around. "And where *is* Chloe, anyway?"

Even Mrs Lovetofts is trying to frown – it's not something she often does and she looks like she's having a bit of trouble getting the hang of it. Elaine continues, "Now, I hope you'll all enjoy your week of rehearsals before the big night next Friday. Just to make it all a little more fun, there will be an award given to the best young actor at the end of the night."

"Oooh!" Zuzanna says. "I do like awards."

"The best young actor." Bianca smiles. "How exciting. I wonder who will win?" she says, although she doesn't sound as if she's really wondering much. "So what's your play about?" she says, turning to me.

Actually, I'm not really that sure what it's about yet. Except it definitely isn't about a fish putting a smell on anyone. "Oh. Hi. Err. It's about a queen and ... err ... a witch, I think."

"Sounds charming. I love fairy stories."

"What's yours about?" Zuzanna asks.

"Ours is a wonderful, heart-warming story about the Ice Queen – that's me," she smiles, "– whose cold heart is melted by a little puppy. Of course, we're so lucky to have Mr Garrick. He's a genius playwright. We only get the best at Mag Hall."

"Yes. So Chloe's always telling us," I say.

"Chloe?" Bianca says.

"She's around somewhere," I say. "Chloe Clarke. She used to come to your school."

"Chloe Clarke? *That* Chloe Clarke?" Bianca says sharply. Then she smiles again. "Yes. Yes, she did. Err ... Where is she?"

"I don't know. She's sort of disappeared," I say, looking around.

"And ... umm ... What part is she playing?" Bianca says.

"She's playing a queen, as well," Gracie says.

"She's playing a queen? What a coincidence. Two queens in one theatre," Bianca says, and her lip twitches a bit. "Girls. Did you hear? Chloe Clarke is here. You remember her, don't you?"

Lavender looks a bit surprised, Naemah looks at her feet. Edwina sneezes. They all seem a bit uncomfortable. All except Willow, who says, "Who's Chloe Clarke?"

"She used to come to our school, Willow. Before you started. I'm afraid she had to lea— I mean ... she left."

I think it's very odd. I'm sure Bianca was about to say Chloe *had to leave*. I wonder why.

"Why?" Willow asks, helpfully.

"You do ask a lot of questions, Willow," Bianca says. "That's not how Mag Hall girls behave."

"Really? Well how do you find things out?" Willow asks.

"Willow. You're doing it again," Bianca snaps. She turns to me. "So what part are you playing?"

"I ... I have a background role," I say, but Bianca doesn't seem to be listening any more. She is looking around the reception area.

Elaine, the theatre manager, claps her hands, making her pink and turquoise hair bounce.

"If you're all ready," she says, "follow me and I'll show you around." She walks off through a pair of double doors and

Mr Garrick follows on with the Mag Hall girls behind.

"Come along everyone," Mrs Lovetofts says, hurrying after them.

"But where's Chloe?" Zuzanna asks.

"I'm just here," Chloe says, stepping out from behind a pillar at the side of the lobby. "Where did you think I was?"

"But what were you doing hiding behind there?" I say as we follow along behind Mrs Lovetofts.

"Hiding? Don't be silly, Emily. I was just ... admiring the architecture. Have you seen those lovely Roman arches?"

"They're water pipes, not Roman arches," Zuzanna says, looking up at the ceiling.

"Magnificent, aren't they?" Chloe says.

Zuzanna eyes her suspiciously. "Mag Hall are here," she says as we go through

the doors to the auditorium. "Don't you want to see your old school friends?"

"Mag Hall? Really? What a surprise," Chloe says.

"Yes. There's a girl called Bianca who knows you."

"Oh, look at that fabulous stage!" Chloe says.

"And some other girls, too – Lavender, Naem—"

"Don't talk to me now – I'm just taking it all in," Chloe says.

The theatre seems huge, rows of seats sweep upwards away from a real stage which has red velvet curtains with gold fringes – they certainly don't look like curtains with health and safety issues. I am suddenly feeling very nervous. I don't think our normal sort of school play is going to fit in here very well.

Elaine stops in front of the stage. "As you can see, this is our beautiful auditorium and this is the stage where you will be performing. Each school

has their own dressing room
and your teachers and I have
just made a rehearsal schedule, so
you can share the stage time."

"I did suggest that Jupiter Road could use the stage today, as we have our own theatre at Magnolia Hall and we've been rehearsing for weeks. But Mrs Lovetofts informs me that you still aren't ready to start rehearsals yet," Mr Garrick says in a "how very concerning" sort of way.

"It's *Juniper* Road," Mrs Lovetofts says. "And the children get the scripts this afternoon. We would have given them out sooner, but the photocopier got jammed and Mrs Brace is the only one who knows how to unjam it and of course she was off with a cold—"

"Oh dear, oh dear. It all sounds most disorganised," Mr Garrick says. "Still, we can use the time to check out the acoustics for our grand finale."

Wow. They have a grand finale, with acoustics, whatever they are. We don't even have an ordinary finale, or a begin-ale. In fact, we don't even have a play yet.

"Why don't you stay and watch?" Mr Garrick says to us. "It would be good to perform in front of an audience, wouldn't it, ladies?"

"What a wonderful idea," Mrs Lovetofts says. "Everyone! Go and take a seat in the auditorium. Thank you, Mr Garrick, you are very kind."

I'm not sure Mr Garrick is being kind. In fact I think Zuzanna's right that he's a big show-off. Still, I go to sit down a couple of rows back from the stage and nearly trip over a small blonde person who is kneeling down behind the seats. "Chloe! What are you doing there?"

"Who? Me? Err ... I'm just looking for my earring."

"It's in your ear," I say.

"I mean the other one."

"That's in the other ear."

"Oh, good. Well spotted, Emily. I could have been looking for hours," she says, finally sitting down.

A few minutes later, Bianca walks on stage in a sparkling robe and glittering silver tiara and announces, "I am the Ice Queen and I have frozen the land!"

The chorus of littlees comes on in the background, dressed in sparkly silver. They are very cute in their little dresses and headbands. They do a sort of ballet dance around Bianca and twinkle in the lights.

Naemah narrates the story of the queen whose heart has turned to ice after her prince was killed in a shipwreck. *It might be very sad for the queen*, I think, *but actually it's quite handy as they haven't got any boys to play the prince anyway.*

"This land will remain cold for ever, like my

frozen heart!" says the queen, and Lavender and Edwina and Willow come on and do a snowflake dance in lacy white dresses – all twirling and whirling about. Well, Lavender and Edwina twirl and whirl, Willow sort of plods, but she does it with a smile. Eventually, the Ice Queen's heart is melted by the present of a small puppy and the land comes back to life again.

There is a grand finale with Bianca, holding a toy puppy, followed by Willow, now dressed as a page boy, carrying her robe. Edwina and Lavender form a sort of angelic chorus going "Ahhhh," in the background. All the littlees dance around dressed as flowers and Bianca does a solo of "White Christmas" (which is a bit odd given that all the snow has just melted, but it's only ever me who notices that sort of thing) and the curtains close.

"Awesome," Gracie says.

"Awesome," Babette says.

"Awesome," Small Emily B. says.

I am just trying to think of another word for "awesome" when the curtains swish open again and we have to clap as all the girls take a bow. I notice that Chloe is not clapping at all, not even one clap, not even with one hand.

"Thank you, thank you," says Mr Garrick, striding on to the stage. "Of course, we need to tweak a few minor details but on the whole we are rather pleased. And of course, we're just dying to see your play, too, Jupiter Road."

"It's *Juniper*," Mrs Lovetofts says.

"Goodbye," Mr Garrick calls as we head back towards the door. "And good luck with the photocopier."

CHAPTER 6

Goggling Grans and Finnish Food

"This is going to be a disaster," Zuzanna says as we trudge back up the road to school. "Actors, singers, and tiny ballet dancers. How can we compete with that?"

"It's not supposed to be a competition," I say.

"Oh wake up, Emily," Chloe says. "Of course it's a competition. You want our school to be the best,

89

don't you? And you want *someone* from our school to win the Best Young Actor Award?"

"You mean you?"

"Of course I mean me. No one else is going to win it for us, are they? Bianca Digby-Cooke obviously thinks it has her name written on it."

"But they're so good already," Zuzanna says.

"I know. At Mag Hall they have dance lessons with Darcey Bussell," Chloe says.

"Why exactly did you leave Mag Hall, Chloe?" Zuzanna says.

"Oh. You know. Stuff."

"But what sort of stuff? Bianca didn't seem sure, either."

"Huh. Bianca Digby-Cooke always has problems remembering things correctly," Chloe says. "I think it's because her bun is too tight. Come on, let's hurry up. I'm freezing." She rushes on ahead, leaving Zuzanna and me behind.

Back at school we have half an hour before lunch and Mrs Lovetofts says we have to "put our thinking caps on", as we're going to do some work on the school anti-bullying policy. This does not seem very fair as I'm sure that writing policies is Mr Meakin's job. I mean, what else do head teachers do all day, except hand out Head Teacher awards in an attempt to make themselves more popular? I should tell my mum – she says using child labour is awful and she won't buy clothes from shops that exploit children. Doesn't stop her getting me to put the washing out, though.

"Who can think of something that we should include in the anti-bullying policy?" Mrs Lovetofts asks.

"Always tell an adult if you are being bullied," Gracie says.

"Good," Mrs Lovetofts says, writing on the board. "Bullies rely on people being too scared to speak up."

"Keep an eye on younger children and report it if you think they are having a problem," says Small Emily B.

"Excellent," Mrs Lovetofts says. "If we all stick together, then bullies can't cause us a problem."

I am not saying anything because the only thing that comes into my head is "Tell Amy-Lee to stop picking on people," and I can't say that or she'll start picking on me.

"Go to a nice school, with nice people," Chloe says, "instead of a rubbish one with bullies in." Amy-Lee spins round in her chair to see if Chloe is talking about her. Luckily, the bell goes before they can get into another row or Chloe can tell everyone that at Mag Hall they had anti-bullying advice from the chief constable of the Metropolitan Police and the head of ChildLine.

At lunch, Chloe is practising being royal all the time. She gets very annoyed when Joshua won't put his coat over a puddle for her to walk across. "Next time I'll have you thrown into the Cupboard of Caretaker," she calls after him.

"The what?" I ask.

"It's a bit like the Tower of London, but more convenient," she says. "Now, hand me the royal lunchbox, will you, I want to eat my majestic macaroon and stately sandwich."

We sit on the ENDSHIP SEA, which used to be mine and Bella's favourite bench to sit on before she moved away and found a Welsh bench instead, and Zuzanna comes to join us.

"She sat down and opened her lunchbox carefully," Zuzanna says.

"Who did?" I ask, looking around.

"She regarded her lunch and tried to decide whether to start with a ham sandwich or perhaps a small apple."

"What are you talking about, Zuzanna?"

"I'm practising for my narrator role," Zuzanna says. "I'm doing everything in the third person ... she said."

I sigh. There's no point talking to either of them. They've both gone play-mad. I suppose I might feel like that if I'd got a good part but the only thing I can do to practise being a rock is to sit still and be quiet, which is not very interesting and makes it very difficult for me to eat my crisps.

All afternoon Mrs Lovetofts seems a bit worried. I'm not sure if it's because of the play but I think it probably is. Either that or she is more upset about the photocopier than she let on.

She puts a map on the whiteboard but does not at all concentrate on what she is doing with her pointer stick and everyone is already writing about the Fjords of Costa Rica before Zuzanna tells her she's pointing to the wrong continent.

"Can anyone tell me where Finland is?" she says after she regains control of her stick. There is an awful lot of quiet.

"I can see I'm going to have to give you a clue," she continues. "Finland is in the north of Europe."

Unfortunately, that is about as helpful as telling me it's close to Narnia.

"Isn't it between Sweden and Russia, Miss?" Zuzanna says.

"Excellent, Zuzanna," Mrs Lovetofts says.

"Boffin," Amy-Lee says.

"No, Baffin Island is over here," Mrs Lovetofts points at the map, "nearer to Greenland. But that

was very good, Amy-Lee. Have a house point for trying."

Amy-Lee looks very confused. Sometimes I think Mrs Lovetofts is from Narnia.

Then Mrs Lovetofts tells us some "interesting" facts about Finland. I don't want to be rude about Finnish people – I'm sure they are really nice – but it is very boring learning about their weather patterns. In fact, this mini-topic is so dull I am almost relieved when Mrs Lovetofts says, "Right, time to give out tonight's homework." Unfortunately, the homework is to find out what people in Finland eat.

Just as the bell goes for the end of school, Mrs Brace bursts in with the play scripts.

"Blessed photocopier! Just needed a kick in the right place," she says, which makes me wonder if there shouldn't be an anti-bullying policy for office machinery, too.

Mrs Lovetofts gives out the scripts and everyone

96

with a speaking part gets all excited and looks at what they have to say. Even people without speaking parts look at when they come on and off stage. I don't bother. As a rock, speaking and moving aren't things that concern me. I am basically an outcast (even though I am in the cast). I put the script in my bag and go home.

Gran and Mum are nattering in the kitchen.

"Hello, love," Mum says. "Good day?"

"Yes, OK," I say. I don't mention the theatre because I don't want to talk about being a rock. I don't mention the mini-topic either, because if I say it's really boring Mum will just start a big lecture on how important all the boring stuff is and then Gran will start on about when she was at school and how they had to learn to do their times tables

backwards with one arm tied behind their back or something.

"Do you know what they eat in Finland?" I say, changing the subject.

"Not really," Mum says. "Fish maybe, or perhaps I'm just thinking that because of the 'Fin' bit ..."

"I know what they eat in Belgium," Gran says. "Chips, that's all. Just chips. With mayonnaise. Not even salad cream. We went there once on a coach trip with the Pensioners' Pilates. You'd have thought they'd have gone somewhere more healthy. Like ... Japan. They have a healthy diet there. Seaweed and tofu. Disgusting, but healthy. Long way on the coach, though—"

"Thanks, Gran," I say quickly, before she starts telling me the story about the Japanese man she met in Morrisons, again. "But the homework is about *Finland*."

"Wait, wait!" Gran says, suddenly getting all

excited. "I'll look it up for you. I can Goggle it." She delves in her handbag and pulls out a phone. "It's a smartyphone!" she says, showing us a shiny new phone with a large screen. "Got it a couple of days ago. The man in the shop says everyone should have one – he gave me a discount because I'm a Silver Skier."

"You mean a Silver Surfer, Gran."

"Oh, no – I'm far too old for that, dear," she says, laughing. "You can Goggle and Faceplace and everything on this. Now then ... Foods of Finland." She taps on the screen with her finger. "Pine trees!" she says.

"What?"

"They eat pine trees, also spruce and birch trees. Goodness, that sounds a bit tough – they must have very good teeth."

"I wonder if you can make soup out of trees," Mum says thoughtfully.

I look over Gran's shoulders. "Gran, you've Goggled, I mean Googled, *Woods* of Finland."

"Oh yes, so I have. Silly me, they make the keyboard so small and fiddly. I'll try again."

"No, Gran, honestly, it's fine. I'll do it myself," I say.

"Elephants," she says. "Oh wait, I think that's Sweden ... Mrs Pritchard's been there, you know, she likes to show off with her holidays."

"Who's Mrs Pritchard?" Mum asks.

"You know Mrs Pritchard. The one who's got a sausage dog and does the crocheting for the homeless. She was with me when I met that nice Japanese man in Morrisons ... "

I slip out, leaving Gran trying to convince Mum that she really does know Mrs Pritchard – perhaps she should just Goggle her. I decide to get my homework over and done with while Gran is keeping Mum occupied – once she gets away she'll start trying to get me to fold the washing or something.

According to the internet, people from Finland eat mostly berries, fish and reindeer, although I bet they actually just have beans on toast like everyone else. Still, it doesn't take long to write that out and then I am a bit bored again. Clover is sleeping and I am not going in the kitchen again in case Gran tries to convince me I know Mrs Pritchard, too.

I am just about to put the TV on, when my phone croaks to tell me I have a message. It's Chloe.

OMG. Have you read the play?

Oh, yes. The play. I think I've blanked it from my mind due to the disappointment of being cast as something that could literally be played better by a large stone.

No. Why?

A black cloak!

Sorry?

The queen has to wear a black cloak.
With the hood up! All the way through.
How will my public recognise me?

But don't you wear a robe and crown?

Only for a few minutes at the end. The rest
is black cloak. I'll look like a witch. Oh, the
humiliation. I would rather be a rock!

Really?

Perhaps there's hope! I don't mind wearing a
cloak.

No, of course not. But it's still really tragic.

I suppose I'm going to have to read the play. I dig
the script out of my bag. It's quite short. It's a story
about a witch who steals a crown from a queen,

then puts a spell on her so that she forgets who she is and wanders around in a black cloak for a bit. Then she remembers and the spell is broken and ... well, that's it really. Oh, and there are quite a lot of townsfolk doing country dancing to fill in. Like I said, Mrs Lovetofts' plays are nothing to get excited about. I mean, if it was a proper story the witch would get punished or something to teach her a lesson but Mrs Lovetofts seems to have forgotten that bit. Amy-Lee will just get the wrong message again.

There is no real mention of what the rocks are for. I had hoped that maybe I could at least be a magic rock or even just a rock that gets a passing mention, you know – "Oh look at that rock, isn't it ... rocky." But no. Nothing. I am just background scenery. Like on *Scooby-Doo* when they run past the same picture fifteen times and hope no one will notice. I do get to move a couple of times. When the scene changes the rocks come to the front of the stage and stand together while the country dancers pile on stage behind us. I think this is meant to hide the dancers from the audience so it will be a surprise when they come on. But as there are only two rocks and eight dancers, I don't think it's going to work very well. The rest of the time my main function is to be ignored.

To cheer myself up I go to see if Bella is online.

 Emily says: Hi Bella

Then I remember that I have told her a big lie. What if she can tell I'm lying just by the way I type or something? Bella's really clever like that.

 Bella says: Hi Emily!

I'm trying to keep my mind blank. Do not think about lies.

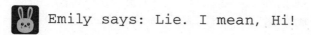

Emily says: Lie. I mean, Hi!

Bella says: I can't believe you.

See! She is a mind reader. She knows.

Emily says: I'm really sorry.

Bella says: I can't believe you didn't tell me that your play is next Friday. That's when we're coming up.

Emily says: Oh no, I won't be able to see you!

Bella says: Don't worry. Mum says we can come to see your play!!!! Auntie Penny has got us tickets!

Emily says: What???

Bella says: Yes – isn't it brill? I'm going to see your starring role!

Emily says: OMG

Bella says: What?

Emily says: OMG. That's amaaaaaaaazing!

Bella says: I know. Sorry, got to go – milking time. But see you soon, Your Majesty!

Disaster! How am I going to be queen by Friday? Wavey Cat – I need you!

CHAPTER 7

All Friends Together ...

Wednesday morning

All night I have been worrying about the play. I had about two minutes' sleep and then I just dreamed about being a queen in a duck costume who got stuck on a table. I have come to the conclusion that my only hope is that Chloe gets struck down with a mystery virus. I want it to be a mystery virus because I don't want her to be very ill. Just have a special sort of illness which makes you unable to do queen things but feel pretty much OK for the rest of the time. I have asked Wavey Cat to help. I feel a bit guilty but it is a total best friend type emergency.

Unfortunately, when I get to school Chloe has not been even a tiny bit struck down. She is looking extremely healthy and queen-ish. She has even persuaded Mrs Lovetofts to let her wear her crown in class. Zuzanna, on the other hand, is looking rather tired. She has been up all night practising her lines.

"You don't have to learn all your lines straight away," Chloe says. "*You* don't have to learn them at all really. Narrators are allowed to read from scripts, aren't they? It's only people with real speaking parts, like me, who have to do all the hard work." She does a sort of look off into the distance and sighs, as if she's endured a lot already.

"Thank you, Chloe, but I pride myself on my professionalism," Zuzanna says. "How about your words, have you learned *any*?"

"After the black cloak revelation last night, I found it very difficult to continue studying the script. However, I have now come to terms with the fact that sometimes an actor has to suffer for her art. If the part demands a black cloak then a black cloak will be worn!"

"Have you got one, then?" I say.

"Not yet," she says. "Black cloaks don't figure very highly in my wardrobe. But I have brought a robe for the last scene when I finally get to wear queen stuff."

"That's just an old pink towel," Zuzanna says, as Chloe pulls a piece of fabric from her bag and swishes it around her shoulders.

"It may have been a towel once," Chloe says, "but when I am on that stage, all people will see is a queen in a golden crown with flowing royal robes.

That's the skill of a true actor, Zuzanna. Anyway, it was the only thing I could find at short notice."

At ten o'clock we set off for the theatre and arrive just as Elaine is unlocking the doors. "Welcome, welcome!" she says, with a broad smile. "Follow me and I'll show you through to your dressing rooms."

Dressing rooms! It all sounds very professional. We walk down a long corridor and emerge at the bottom of some steps.

"They're just along here," Elaine says. "And the stage is just up those steps."

I get a little thrill of excitement and nerves. Next week we will be standing on that stage in front of a big audience. Then I remember that one of the big audience will be Bella and my excitement turns

to worry, which is basically the story of my life anyway.

"Which dressing room is mine?" Chloe asks.

"This is your school's girls' dressing room and that's the boys', just a little further along," Elaine says. "Magnolia Hall's dressing rooms are at the end of the corridor – one for the big girls and one for the littlees."

"But which one is mine? Does it have a star on the door yet?" Chloe asks.

Elaine looks a little confused and runs her hand through her turquoise and pink quiff. "I'm sorry, we don't have enough dressing rooms for everyone to have their own. I'm afraid you all have to share," she says.

"*Share*?" Chloe says. "I'll bet this never happens to Angelina Jolie." She closes her eyes and starts doing her Darth Vader breathing again.

Elaine goes down the corridor and lets the boys into their room and then comes back to open ours.

All the girls pile in. It isn't what I expected. It's not at all glamorous. It's small and smells of flowery air freshener with a background hint of mould. There is a big dressing table with a long mirror on one wall, and five chairs and clothes hooks along the other. There are a few odd pieces of old clothing and costumes hanging around. Everything looks a bit grubby.

"Shove up a bit," Amy-Lee says from behind me. I shuffle forward but there's not really much room. I don't see how we're ever going to all fit in and get changed.

"Do move up, girls," Mrs Lovetofts says. "Half of us are still in the corridor."

Somebody pushes me from behind and I stumble forward.

"Hey, you're on my foot," Gracie says. "Get your big hooves off!"

"Sorry," I say. "It's just that everyone's shoving me."

"This is impossible," Chloe says. "I am virtually like the meat in a Year Six sandwich, which is certainly not how royalty should be treated."

"Perhaps it would help if you thought of yourself as smoked salmon," I say, but Chloe doesn't seem to appreciate my attempt to cheer her up.

"Oh dear," Elaine says from the doorway. "It's a bit of a squash, isn't it? Perhaps we need a rethink. I'll tell you what, the Magnolia Hall girls have got a bigger room – because they were here first they chose the best one – but if a few of you don't mind sharing ... "

"Oh, yes please, Elaine," Mrs Lovetofts says. "Anything's better than this. Yasmin, will you please be careful where you put your elbow? Your coat is very nice but I don't want to taste it. Now, who have I got who's sensible ...? Zuzanna, Emily and Chloe, can you go with Elaine, please?"

Sometimes being sensible can get you into a whole load of problems.

"Oh ... err ... I'm just going to the toilet. I'll catch you up," Chloe says and runs off in the other direction.

Zuzanna and I follow Elaine down the corridor to another room. On the door is a handwritten sign: *Mag Hall. Keep Out!* Someone has drawn a skull and crossbones underneath it.

Elaine laughs. "Those Magnolia Hall girls love a little joke! They are a fun bunch." She opens the door to reveal a room pretty much like the last one but a bit bigger and with eight tatty chairs instead of five.

"Well, ladies, make yourselves at home. You can see which chairs the other girls are using so if you just put your things on those spare ones over there I'm sure you'll all get on fine."

She goes out quickly, closing the door behind her, before I even have time to finish thinking, *I'm not sure this is a very good idea.*

There's a creak as the door opens again, very

slightly, and a cardboard crown peeps round followed by a pair of eyes.

"Oh. No one here then," Chloe says and straightens up, pushing the door open.

"As we have rehearsals at different times we probably won't see much of the Mag Hall girls," Zuzanna says. "Which will be a pity for you as you haven't seen much of them at all yet, have you?" She narrows her eyes suspiciously. "Anyone would think you were trying to avoid them."

"Why on earth would I do that?" Chloe snaps.

"Everyone on stage, please," Mrs Harris says, sticking her head round the door. "Chop, chop and get a move on."

I don't like Mrs Harris saying "chop, chop" – when she looks at me, I think she might mean it literally.

115

CHAPTER 8

Comedy of Errors

Still Wednesday morning

We hurry down the corridor to the stairs where everyone is queuing to go up. My stomach is doing flip flops and my knees feel sort of watery. I don't know why I'm so nervous, it's not like there's anyone to watch us. Still, I feel quite trembly as I climb the stairs behind Chloe and emerge at the side of the stage.

Chloe starts doing her breathing thing again. "Oh, I'm just not feeling it," she says.

"Feeling what?" Zuzanna asks.

"Feeling the part, feeling royal. Ah good, here are my servants," she says as Nicole and Babette come up the steps.

"Ladies-in-waiting," Babette snaps. "Ladies-in-waiting were quite important too, you know? They weren't just servants."

"That's obviously not true," Chloe says. "If they were important they wouldn't have had to do all that waiting about, would they?"

"Could I have the queen, please?" Mrs Harris calls from the front of the stage. "Are you there, Chloe?"

"Just a minute," Chloe says. "I forgot my robe."

"It's a towel," Zuzanna says as Chloe disappears off down the stairs again.

"Where's Chloe now?" Mrs Lovetofts says, stepping into the wings.

"She'll be right back," I say. "Costume issue."

She sighs and walks back out on to the stage. "Slight technical hitch," she calls to Mrs Harris, who is watching from the auditorium.

"Technical hitch?" Mrs Harris says. "How can we have a technical hitch – we haven't even started yet! Oh, never mind. Let's get the rocks on stage."

"Could we have our rocks, please?" Mrs Lovetofts calls.

"That's you," Zuzanna says, giving me a shove.

I can't believe I'm going to be first out. I walk nervously on to the stage. Mrs Harris glares at me from the front row. "Oh. It's Emily Sparkes," she says.

Chop chop, I think. I bite my lip and look away, out into the auditorium. The theatre looks three times as big from up here. There are bright lights shining from the ceiling and rows and rows of seats

and ... hang on ... there are some people sitting out there. An audience! I freeze.

"Excellent, Emily, not moving a muscle. You look very rock-like!" Mrs Lovetofts says. "Now if you could just move a little further back – the rocks are meant to be at the back of the stage. Emily. Emily?"

My feet feel like they are stuck to the floor. I can't move my legs – it's like when I got table fright all over again.

"Emily Sparkes. MOVE!" Mrs Harris yells.

I stumble back towards the rear of the stage. Someone in the audience giggles. I try to stand still like a rock but now my knees are shaking and if your knees shake then the rest of you can't help but do the same. Gross-Out

comes on and stands at
the other side of the stage.
He is nothing like a rock, either.
Not because he is nervous but because he
finds it impossible to keep still for more than
a couple of seconds. He keeps scratching his head
(he's probably got nits) and poking his finger in
his ear (I have never heard of ear nits, but if they're
available, he's probably got them too). Anyone
watching this play will be wondering why there's
a minor earthquake going on in the background.

"Emily and Gavin, you do realise that rock refers
to what you are and not what you do? Now keep
still!" Mrs Harris snaps. There's another giggle
from the auditorium. Who are those people out
there? It's really hard to see because the lights are
shining in my eyes. And then there is something
about the light shining in my eyes which makes
me want to—

"Atchoo!"

"Emily Sparkes! When have you ever heard a rock sneeze?"

This time the giggling turns to laughter.

"Ah, I think the queen's ready," Mrs Lovetofts says, quickly.

"And, ACTION!" Mrs Harris shouts. "But obviously not the rocks."

I make my very best effort to stop my knees shaking.

Zuzanna stands at the side of the stage and says, "Once, there was a queen who was having a bad day."

Chloe walks regally on to the stage with her towel round her shoulders. It's very long, and Nicole and Babette walk on behind her, sulkily holding it off the ground.

"CUT," Mrs Harris says. "Why are the ladies-in-waiting on stage? You're not in this scene. The queen has lost her memory, she has forgotten she's a queen. Also," Mrs Harris continues, "ladies-in-waiting were quite important – they didn't do that sort of thing."

"Told you," Nicole and Babette say together and drop Chloe's towel.

"You're going to have to cast someone as my servant then," Chloe snaps, swirling the cloak around her. "I can't be expected to carry my own robes, can I?"

"You are not supposed to be wearing a robe in this scene, nor a crown," Mrs Harris says.

"I need it to get into character," Chloe says. "How can I be expected to act, without the right props?"

"Perhaps she could keep it on just for this rehearsal," Mrs Lovetofts says, with a pleading look towards Mrs Harris. "Let's try again."

"ACTION," Mrs Harris says, scowling.

"Once, there was a queen who was having a bad day," Zuzanna reads again.

 "Oh dear, why am I wandering about in this forest?" Chloe says in her best queen-ish type voice. "I've lost my memory. Like, totally."

She looks forlornly out into the audience. Mrs Harris makes a bit of a growly noise.

"Err . . . STOP . . . or do I mean CUT . . . or is that just for films?" Mrs Lovetofts says.

Mrs Harris's growly noise is getting louder.

"Anyway," Mrs Lovetofts says quickly. "That was lovely, Chloe dear, but the words 'like, totally' are not in the script."

"I know that. I'm ad-libbing – it's what all the best actors do."

"If you could just stick to the script for now," Mrs Lovetofts smiles, "it might be a little less confusing."

Chloe sucks in her cheeks and repeats in a much less queen-ish way, "I've lost my memory."

Then it goes a bit quiet. No one seems to know what is supposed to happen next.

"Witch," Mrs Harris says in a loud whisper.

"Which what?" Chloe whispers back. There are more girly giggles from the audience.

"Which nothing," Mrs Harris says. "Where's the witch?"

"Which witch?" calls someone from the audience and there's lots more giggling and a sort of snorty man's laugh. And then I realise who is watching. It's the Mag Hall girls and Mr Garrick. How come they're here already? It's supposed to be our turn.

There is a bit of shuffling at the side of the stage and then Amy-Lee appears.

"That's which witch," calls someone from the audience and they shriek with laughter.

"Oi. Audience. Shut it," Amy-Lee says.

"CUT!" Mrs Harris yells. She paces up and down in front of the stage. "Can we just try to stick to the script, please? Let's start from the beginning. Again. Perhaps this time we could get past the first line."

Zuzanna says, "Once, there was a queen who was having a bad day."

"I know how she feels," Mrs Harris mutters.

"Oh dear, why am I wandering about in this forest?" Chloe says. "I have so totally lost my memory and I don't even have a servant to carry my train."

Mrs Harris puts her head in her hands.

"Heh heh heh!" Amy-Lee laughs, leaping on to the stage. "Maybe I can help!" She makes a very good witch, although I'm not sure how much acting she's doing, really.

"And then you wave your wand around in the air twice and tap the queen on the arm," Mrs

Lovetofts says, as Mrs Harris is still hiding behind her hands. Amy-Lee waves her magic wand enthusiastically but just as she's about to tap Chloe's arm, Chloe gets her toe caught in her flowing towel and stumbles forward. Amy-Lee's wand flicks Chloe on the back of the head instead and the cardboard crown goes flying off into the audience.

"Cut. Cut!" calls Mrs Harris, but no one can hear her over the shrieking of the Mag Hall audience.

"You did that on purpose!" Chloe says to Amy-Lee.

"It's not my fault you're dragging an old towel around," Amy-Lee says.

"That's why I need servants to carry my train," Chloe says. "That could have been a major royal health and safety incident!"

"CUT!" Mrs Harris says.

"Perhaps we should take a break," Mrs Lovetofts says. "It's been a busy morning."

"Tea up!" Elaine calls, pushing a tea trolley into the auditorium. "I'm sure the teachers could do with a cup."

"Just water for me. I'm off tea," Mrs Harris says, giving me a hard stare as I hurry off stage.

Back in the dressing room Chloe is having a strop. "Working with amateurs is so difficult," she says. "How am I supposed to play royalty with no one to boss around?"

"If it's all getting too much for you, Chloe, I'm willing to let you have my rock role," I say, hopefully.

"Emily, do you really think I would give up my starring role to play a lump of—"

She doesn't get any further because the dressing room door opens and Elaine walks in with

Bianca, closely followed
by Lavender, Edwina and
Naemah, with Willow tagging
along behind.

Edwina sneezes twice and I cross my fingers and hope she stands close to Chloe.

"As I was explaining, ladies," Elaine says, looking over Bianca's shoulder, "we need to share dressing rooms now that Juniper Road are here too. I'm sure you'll all get on wonderfully." She smiles brightly. "I hope it's not too much of a squash."

Bianca smiles back. "I'm sure we'll manage, Elaine. Thank you."

Elaine bustles out, saying, "Such lovely girls," and closes the door behind her.

"Well, this is fun," Bianca says. "I have to say we loved your play, didn't we, girls? I especially adore comedy, it's such an inspired choice."

"Really funny," Lavender says. "We couldn't stop laughing."

"Oh. I don't think it was meant to be a comedy ..." Willow says and then trails off as Bianca shoots her a look.

"And you were such a brilliant rock, Emily."

"Really?" I say.

"Yes. I think it's quite a difficult part. All that standing still. It takes a lot of concentration."

"Thanks," I say. "Most people don't understand that," and I can't help feeling a little bit proud.

"You too, Zuzanna, great reading." Bianca smiles and Zuzanna smiles back.

"And Chloe. Nice to see you again. How are you getting on now?"

"Fine," Chloe says, and she turns away and starts fiddling with her bag.

Bianca looks a bit hurt. "Oh. Well. I'm sure we're all really glad to hear that you've put your problems behind you, aren't we, girls?" The other girls sort of mutter "Yes," and Naemah looks at her feet again.

"I'm sorry, Chloe, I don't know you," says Willow

brightly. "But then I only started last week so everything before that is a mystery to me! Ha ha—"

"Willow," Bianca interrupts sharply. "I'm sure the Juniper Road girls don't want to hear your entire life story."

"Oh. Sorry," Willow says and bites her lip.

Bianca turns back to us. "Willow's new. She's still getting used to how things work at our school, aren't you, Willow?"

"Yes, I am. Just call me Newbie!" Willow laughs.

"Oh. And I need to give this back," Bianca says and she pulls out a very squashed cardboard crown. "That was such a funny idea to make it fly off into the audience. Pity, though, it's got so crushed." She smiles and puts Chloe's crown on the table. Unfortunately, it has got very tattered and battered. It almost looks as if someone's jumped up and down on it.

Elaine bangs on the door. "Juniper Road, back on stage please."

Chloe grabs her crown from Bianca, smooths it out and balances it on her head. She wraps her scraggy towel around her and hurries out. Zuzanna and I follow.

"See you later," Bianca says as we close the door.

Zuzanna is scowling at Chloe as we walk up the corridor. "Chloe, you were quite rude to Bianca. She's only trying to be friendly."

"Zuzanna, I'm getting into character," Chloe says. "Do you mind?" and she does loud breathing so that she can't hear anyone speaking.

"There's definitely something going on there," Zuzanna says to me. "Why is Chloe being so offish with the Mag Hall girls? It's embarrassing."

She frowns a 4.2 and for once it's not my fault.

The rest of the rehearsal is almost as bad as the earlier bit. Alfie forgets to come on and when Chloe says, "Pray tell me, where is the innkeeper?" someone shouts from the wings, "He's in the toilet!" and we all have to wait till he comes out. Then Nicole and Babette get into a row on stage about who is the best lady-in-waiting and Yeah-Yeah Yasmin forgets her line even though it's just "Yeah."

At least the Mag Hall girls aren't in the audience this time. Apparently they are doing their hair and make-up ready for their rehearsal. I can't believe they are doing dress rehearsals that need hair and make-up, when half of our cast can't even remember which character they are yet.

"Well done, everyone!" Mrs Lovetofts claps as the rehearsal ends. "A few teething problems but I'm sure it'll all be all right on the night! Don't you think, Mrs Harris?"

"If we get a Christmas miracle," mutters Mrs Harris.

CHAPTER 9

Action Plans!

Friday afternoon

We have been practising our play all week and it is still absolutely a disaster.

On Thursday morning Joshua's trousers split during the country dancing and he had to dance off stage sideways (which happens quite a lot in country dancing so I suppose it wasn't too bad, except for the people standing behind him who got the full view of his ancient Spider-Man underpants). On Thursday afternoon, Yeah-Yeah Yasmin leaned on the scenery and a cardboard tree landed on Amy-Lee and squashed her witch's hat. Then, this morning we had no one to play the witch because Amy-Lee had to stay outside Mr Meakin's office for what she did to Yasmin for squashing her witch's hat. Plus, nobody ever remembers their lines. Well, no one except Zuzanna and she's the only one who doesn't need to because she's allowed to read from the script. Most people haven't even got a costume yet, even though Mrs Harris has been going on at them all week. She says if we don't all know our lines by Monday she's resigning as Mrs Lovetofts' assistant. I think that was one of the few times I've ever seen Mrs Lovetofts stop smiling. On top of everything I've got a cold. I don't know if Wavey Cat has made a mistake with the mystery virus, or if I stood too close to Edwina, but Mrs Harris gets very irritable when one of her rocks sneezes. Unfortunately, Chloe is still totally mystery-virus free.

We arrive back at school after rehearsal feeling very gloomy. "It's so embarrassing. Juniper Road is going to look so useless in front of everyone," Zuzanna says. "Mag Hall's play is so much better. Bianca is really good."

"*I'm* really good!" Chloe says. "It's just the material I have to work with. Have you any idea how difficult it is to make Mrs Lovetofts' script

 work? Really, this is one of the greatest challenges of my acting career," she sighs.

"Chloe, you're ten. You're at school. You haven't got a career," Zuzanna says.

"You know nothing of the world of show business," Chloe says. "I'm just resting, in case I suffer from child-star burnout."

"Girls," I say, doing my peacekeeper bit, "none of this is helping us with the play."

"True. What we need is a plan," Chloe says.

"A plan?" I say, holding open the classroom door for Chloe to walk regally through. (It's become a habit now.)

"Yes, like when we had to make your mum Britain's Best Mum – that plan worked, didn't it?"

"Err ... no, not really."

"Well it sort of worked and a sort of working plan is better than the plan we've

got now which is a sort of no plan, working or not working," Chloe says and then looks a bit puzzled, like she might have confused herself as well as everyone else.

"I don't think a sort of any plan is going to save us," Zuzanna says.

"Well, I for one am not willing to stand by and let Bianca Digby-Cooke win the best actor award," Chloe says.

"You have really got it in for her, haven't you?" Zuzanna says. "What exactly went on between you two at Mag Hall?"

"Zuzanna, I am trying to save the reputation of our school. I would appreciate your support. Now, as usual, you're in charge of writing things."

Zuzanna sighs and picks up her NV Boyz pencil case. "Fine, at least it gives me a chance to use my new scented gel pens," she says. "I think I'll go

for coconut, it's quite a sensible scent. I always think mango and pineapple are a bit silly. Quite nice for birthday cards, but not lists."

"Right. What's better about their play than ours?" Chloe says.

"Everything," I say.

"Helpful as ever, Emily. But perhaps you could be a bit more specific."

"Costumes."

"Good. Write that down. Get better costumes. What else?"

"The dancing."

"We can work on that."

"The actors."

"*Some* of the actors," Chloe says.

"The grand finale. Like, they have one and

we don't. Oh, and the scenery of course, we only had a cardboard tree and Amy-Lee's broken that."

"Details, details," Chloe says. "OK. Let's see the list."

Better Play List

1. Get better costumes
2. Get better dancers
3. Get better actors
4. Get some, not broken, scenery
5. Get a grand finale

"Well, that's only five things. I'm sure we can manage five things," Chloe says.

"In five days?" Zuzanna says.

"Plus the weekend, Zuzanna. Do try to be positive. Let's get started right away. Everyone needs to learn their lines this weekend."

"That's fine for us, but how are we going to get

the rest of the class to do it? Alfie Balfour just makes it up as he goes along," Zuzanna says.

"Yes, that's true," I say. "Today, when Chloe said, 'Innkeeper, do you have somewhere I can stay for the night?' he said, 'Have you tried the Premier Inn?'"

"Good point. We need to get everyone to promise – give me a pen. A very serious pen."

"Hmm," Zuzanna says. "This calls for … plum – I always think plums are very intelligent."

"Excellent." Chloe rips a bit of paper out of the back of my Literacy book.

"Hey, don't do that! I'll get in trouble."

"Emily, we are dealing with a serious situation here. Emergency measures need to be taken."

"Well next time take emergency measures out of your own book," I say, snatching my book back and stuffing it in my bag.

Chloe holds up the bit of paper to show us.

I, the person signing this bit of paper, promise you, the person holding this bit of paper, that I will:
  a) Learn all my lines
  b) Get a decent costume
  c) Become an expert country dancer
By the end of this weekend.
Sign below:

....

"But just because they've signed it doesn't mean they'll do it," I say.

"I know. What they need is some gentle persuasion. Now where's my co-star?" Chloe says.

"Co-star?"

"Amy-Lee. If ever there was a girl good at

143

persuading people to do what she wants, it's Amy-Lee."

"It's lunchtime. She'll be outside Mr Meakin's office on detention."

"Good point. I'll go and see her."

A couple of minutes later Chloe is back. Amy-Lee has added a line to the bottom of the page.

Anyone not learning their lines will have me to answer to. This may include broken rulers or punctured footballs. Just sayin. Amy-Lee.

"Amy-Lee's very keen on beating Mag Hall since they heckled her." Chloe smiles. "Sign, please."

"I'm sure this is against the anti-bullying policy," Zuzanna says, frowning as she scribbles her name.

By the end of the afternoon Chloe has a full list

of signatures from everyone in the class. She and Amy-Lee have bonded in a very alarming way and give each other scary smiles every time someone signs. It's like watching the formation of a new, evil empire, with plaits.

Chloe is feeling very pleased with herself as we walk out of school.

"I think we'll see a vast improvement by Monday."

"What about the scenery?" I say. "Have you got a plan for that?"

"Err ... no. In fact I thought I'd leave that one to you, Emily. I see you as the expert in that area."

"Me?"

"Yes. I mean after all you're basically playing a piece of scenery, aren't you?"

Oh, great. Just when I've got enough to worry about I now have to sort the scenery, too.

"But you're always telling me I'm rubbish at art," I call, but Chloe is already heading out of the gate.

I walk home with Zuzanna, who is still very keen to talk about Chloe. "What do you think her problems were at Mag Hall?" she says.

"I don't know. Maybe she didn't like the school dinners."

"Don't be silly, Emily," Zuzanna says. "It's something more personal than that. She doesn't seem to be very nice to Bianca, does she?"

I let Zuzanna chatter on about Chloe as we walk, but really all I can think about is how I'm going to get to be the queen by Friday. The whole mystery-virus thing has completely backfired. I have been sneezing all day. *I need another plan.*

"Another plan for what?" Zuzanna says.

I must have said it out loud. The stress is clearly

beginning to affect me. "Umm. Another plan for ... my costume. Not just T-shirt and leggings."

"I'm not sure there's a lot you can do with a rock," Zuzanna says. "I don't think I've ever seen an interesting one."

CHAPTER 10

How to Make a Scene

Saturday morning

On Saturday morning I make the mistake of standing in the kitchen for thirty seconds. This is all the time it takes for Mum to decide I need a job and she hands me the washing basket.

"Just pop those on the line for me, love," she says, with one of those innocent Mum smiles.

"But I've got a cold," I sniff.

"Well the fresh air will do you good. Look, the sun's shining. Better make the most of it," she says, shoving me towards the door.

Staggering down the path with a massive basket of wet clothes and a bag of pegs stuffed under my chin doesn't really feel much like "making the most of it" to me.

I must be doing a lot of huffing because after a couple of minutes a dark head pokes through the hole in the hedge.

"Hi," Lena says. "You're doing a lot of sighing for a Saturday."

"I've got a lot to sigh about," I sigh. "I've got all this play stuff to sort out, I've got a cold and my weekend is being wasted with washing."

Lena wriggles through the hole. "I would help you put the washing out," she says, "but I think I'm allergic to housework. I once got a rash after hoovering the living room, so best not to chance it ... I might be able to help you with the play, though."

"I need some ideas about scenery," I say. Mag Hall have got all these backdrops and things. We need the stage to look like a forest and at the moment it looks like ... well, like a stage."

"Hmm," Lena says, not very helpfully.

I wrestle a sheet out of the washing basket and try to get it on to the washing line. Unfortunately, it sort of drags through the mud on the way. "The trouble is," I say, trying to brush off the dirt and sort of smearing it around, "I don't know where to start."

"A sheet!" Lena says.

"Yes, Lena. It's a sheet – people put them on beds."

"You look like you're putting that one on a flowerbed," Lena laughs.

"Well, if you'd be more helpful—"

"I am being helpful. Look, a sheet – I mean, that's what you could use for scenery."

"Lena, the queen is lost in a forest, not her bedroom."

"But you could paint it. I'll help you – I love art."

"A painted sheet?"

"Yes, you know, to use as a backdrop. Maybe more than one – we could do a few."

"Hmm ... that's actually a really good idea," I say. "There's loads of paint in the shed and I'm sure Mum will let me have some old sheets. In fact," I say, looking at the mud, "I think this one's a bit scruffy."

"See, just call me Lena the Gena–ius."

"Just stick to art, Lena. Poetry is definitely not your thing."

Mum's a bit grumpy about the muddy sheet but in the end she lets me have it and finds a couple more. Lena and I spread them out in the back garden and draw big trees on two of them with a marker pen before painting them brown and green. Then Lena paints another one to look like the inside of a castle with stone walls and an arched window for the final scene.

"These are amazing, Lena," I say, looking at the sheets drying in the sun. "You should be our Artistic Director!"

"Do you think they'd let me?" Lena says. "Help, I mean? I'd really like to be backstage."

"I think they'll take all the help they can get. Let's ask Mrs Lovetofts on Monday."

I manage to be quite pleased with everything for about five minutes, then I remember the play promises. I dig out the signed sheet. I need to:

a) Learn all my lines

b) Get a decent costume

c) Become an expert country dancer

Luckily, the first bit doesn't apply to me as I haven't got any lines to learn, and I also don't have to practise the country dancing because there is no such thing as a dancing rock, but I need to do something about my costume, or my ruler will not be safe from Amy-Lee. I really like my ruler. Gran got it for me on one of her "Old People Visit Even Older Things" coach trips to a stately home. It has all the kings and queens of England in order, so it's a ruler ruler. See? Once, when Dad was trying to find the snooker on BBC Two we accidentally ended up watching *University Challenge*. The man asked, "Which monarch succeeded Richard the Third?" And I looked at my ruler ruler and said, "Henry the Seventh." Dad couldn't believe it – he said I was a genius child and should go to Cambridge University. I was very pleased but I'm not sure if they do camel-whispering courses.

I do not feel very clever at the moment. I am not really sure how I'm going to make my costume super amazing by Monday morning. There's really not a lot you can do with a grey T-shirt and leggings. I lay them out on the bed and have a think. I try scrumpling them up a bit to see if I can make them look a bit more rocky, but they just look like a wrinkled up T-shirt and leggings. Apart from sticking actual rocks all over them I can't really think of anything, and I don't think Pritt Stick works on rocks. My creativityness is at zero. I'm getting a bit worried about it. Lena had all the scenery ideas. I haven't had one bit of creativityness this week. What if it's totally gone? It's the only thing I'm any good at.

I go downstairs to check my advent calendar for any forgotten chocolates (I do this every day but there never seem to be any) and do a bit of general sighing in the hope that someone might notice I'm fed up, but Dad is in the living room watching football so he is not capable of noticing anything else. I find Mum in the kitchen, hiding from the football.

"Mum, I need a better costume. T-shirt and leggings are just not going to cut it in real Theatreland," I say.

"Emily, you're only a rock. I don't think you have to worry too much," she says, then bites her lip and says quickly, "I didn't mean that rocks are not important, of course they are. Rocks are essential to the world. I mean, where would we all be without rocks? Just floating ... in space." She looks a bit desperate.

I sigh. "I know what you mean, Mum, it's not the best part in the world, but we are going to totally let down the school if we don't get some decent costumes. Mag Hall have got a costume designer!"

"Really? Goodness, school has changed since I was young. The best costume I ever got was a bin liner with armholes poked through."

"What was that for?"

"Umm . . . I can't really remember. I think I was a crow. Oh yes, I had to say, 'Caw, caw.'"

So at least I know my rubbish-part problems are inherited.

"Look, if you really want to have a proper rock costume why don't you ask your dad? I'm sure he could do something with an old cardboard box."

An old cardboard box does not sound particularly inspiring but I'm in a desperate situation – my ruler ruler is in peril. I go to find Dad in the living room.

"Dad, could you help me with my rock costume?" I say.

"He dived! You need glasses, ref! Did you see that, Emily?"

"Dad, I need help for the school play."

"Get up off the floor, you big baby! Look at him pretending to be injured. You never see that in snooker."

There is only one thing for it. I stand in front of the TV. It is an act of peaceful protest.

"Emily! Get out of the way— Oh! Now I've missed the penalty."

"Dad, I need some help with my rock costume. It is an important part of my education and, as I am your child, it should be more important than football!"

"Oh all right, Emily, I get it. It's one of those 'prove you're a proper father' things. OK. OK, I'll prove it – after the football. Now please, get out of the way."

Luckily, Dad's team wins so he is very cheerful when the match ends. He comes to find me in my room and gives me a hug. "Did you see that last goal?"

"No Dad, I can't see through floorboards. Although I did hear you shouting."

"It was brilliant – right in the top corner." He tries to demonstrate by kicking one of my school socks across the room but stubs his toe on the bed and has to sit down to recover.

"So what is this rock thing?" he says after he's stopped telling the bed what he thinks of it.

I tell him (again) about the rock costume and he suddenly jumps up and says "Undercoat!" and hobbles out of the room.

A little while later I find him in the shed, painting a cardboard box grey. "Undercoat," he says, indicating the paint tin. "It's grey paint."

After dinner he goes into the living room and starts screwing sheets of newspaper into little balls and kicking them across the room, his toe seems to have recovered. "Dad, you can't play football in here, Mum'll go mad," I say.

"Not footballs, Emily, rocky protrusions," he

says and kicks another newspaper ball on to the pile. "You just leave it to me, by tomorrow you will have a costume fit for a rock star!" He grins at me. "Rock star – get it?"

"Yes Dad," I say. "I get it," although I'm beginning to wonder if the grey leggings and T-shirt might be OK after all.

The next morning Dad gets me up extra early to try on my box, I mean, costume. He's very pleased with himself, like painting a cardboard box is a real achievement.

"It should be dry by now, it's had all night. After you'd gone to bed I stuck the scrunched up newspaper lumps on. What do you think? Gives it a bit more of a rocky texture."

"I think I wish I was the queen," I say.

"Come on, try it on," he says. He holds it over my head. "Just keep still and I'll ... "

Suddenly the world goes dark.

"Great," I hear him say from what sounds like far away.

It is not great, it is very uncomfortable. The box reaches down to my ankles and is sort of balancing on my head. I can't see anything and everything sounds muffly.

"Dad, Dad? Can you get this off me now?" I say. I take a step towards where I think he might be. "Dad. Can you get me out of this?" I am walking like a penguin, I can only do tiny steps and I can't move my arms at all.

"Dad?"

There is a loud crash and Dad says something which I don't quite catch (and that's probably a good thing) and then the world lights up again as he pulls the box off my head.

"Emily, for goodness' sake. Be careful. You knocked the lamp off the table."

"It's not my fault – I can't see a thing! I can't spend the entire play in this. I'll probably get boxophobia or something."

Dad sighs. "I'll cut a hole for you to see out of, hang on."

He takes the box out to the kitchen and I hear some sawing sounds then he brings it back for me to try again.

"There," he says, plopping the box over my head again, "a pretty good job, even if I do say so myself. Meet my daughter, Number One Rock."

"Number Two, actually," I say. "Can you take it off now please?"

Dad lifts off the box and puts it on the table. Then he stands back and admires it like he's a fine craftsman.

Rock That Box

Monday morning

This morning I got up early and ate my Coco-Crispies in record time. This is because I need some peace and quiet and non-crunchy time to concentrate on creativity. I have been concentrating for about five minutes now but I'm still not getting any ideas. What if my creativity has gone for ever? What if telling lies makes creativityness disappear?

The only thing I can think of is to tell Bella on Friday that, at the last minute, I felt too ill to be the queen and Chloe stood in for me. She won't know it's me in the rock box, so I can just pretend I had to stay in the dressing room. Then I'll just have to make sure she doesn't speak to Chloe or anyone after the play. It's not a good solution because it means I'll have lied to her twice – that probably means I'll never get my Emily Sparkes creativityness back. It also means I'm a rubbish friend.

I flick Wavey Cat's paw. "There must be a better solution than this, Wavey Cat. I just wanted a starring role, so Bella would be proud of me, but it's all gone disaster-shaped again!"

My phone croaks. It's Zuzanna.

Going in early. See you at school.

I don't know why she's going in early – she probably wants to find some extra homework to do, she's like that. At least I don't have to walk with her, carrying my rock-box. She'd definitely give that a 4.8 on the frown scale.

Lena and I walk to school. She carries the folded-up scenery sheets and I carry my box costume in a black bin liner, which is very awkward.

"I'll ask Mrs Ahmed if I can help with your play today," she says. "I'm sure she won't mind – we're not really doing any work at the moment and I'm sick of Christmas word searches."

"This box is so awkward," I say, shifting it from one side to the other. "I'm fed up with being a rock."

"Well, I think playing things like a duck and a rock shows you're versatile."

"Versatile?"

"Yeah, you know. Like you can do different things."

"Like what?"

"Well. Umm ... You have to move to be a duck and you have to stay still to be a rock. That shows you can play lots of different roles."

"Yes, maybe," I say. Perhaps she's right. At least I've got a part and get to go on stage in a real live theatre. How many eleven-year-olds get that opportunity? I'm already half way to being a child star and I hadn't realised it. I'm going to be a really good rock. The best rock ever. I could even become famous for it and get asked to play a rock in theatres all over the world.

"Thanks, Lena," I say. "You've really cheered me up."

"Oh, have I? Hmm. Being cheerful isn't really part of my image. Don't tell anyone, will you?"

Lena drops off the scenery sheets in my class and I promise to mention her to Mrs Lovetofts. It was nice of her to say that stuff about me being versatile. *Being a rock is not such a bad part*, I think. Bianca said it took talent as well. And then I have an idea. What if I could convince Chloe that being a rock is better than being a queen? What if I could convince her to swap parts? Move over Plan A, Plan B has arrived!

Zuzanna is in class already, pacing up and down and reading her lines.

"I can't practise at home," she says. "Mum keeps interfering and asking when I'm going to get to the interesting bit. She says it needs more passion and excitement – she watches far too much *Holby City*."

I dump my box in the corner.

"What's that?" Zuzanna asks.

I pull off the bin bag. "It's my new, improved rock costume," I say.

"It looks like a box," Zuzanna says, "with lumps on."

"A rock is not an easy thing to make," I say, feeling a bit defensive of my dad. I struggle to put the bin bag over the box again but it catches on the corner and the bag rips in half.

"Never mind," Zuzanna says. "That's probably a good thing. Someone might have thrown it out with the rubbish."

"Make way for the royal procession." On the other side of the classroom, Chloe has just come through the door and is walking carefully towards us. She is wearing a flowing golden robe and Small Emily B. is walking behind her, trying to stop it dragging along the floor.

"Come on, S. E. B. – pick it up. You'd make a useless bridesmaid."

"I'm supposed to be the innkeeper's wife," Small Emily B. says. "Not your personal assistant."

"I do think standards are slipping," Chloe sighs. "There was a time when people knew how to treat royalty." She comes to a regal halt in front of us. "Good morning, peasants. You'll never guess how I made this fabulous flowing robe," she says, swooshing her golden cape around and sending Small Emily B. flying across the classroom.

"Is it a curtain?" Zuzanna says.

"Well, yes, actually it is. Lucky guess. It's one of my nan's curtains out of her spare room. I don't think she'll notice. She doesn't go in there much."

"It's definitely an improvement on the towel," Zuzanna says. "But you're supposed to be wearing the black cloak until the grand finale."

"Yes, I've been having a think about that. I don't think it's very ... in character."

"What do you mean?" I say, as Chloe pulls something from her bag.

"Well, I thought if a queen has to wear a black cloak it should at least be a bit posh. I mean, she's not going to wear any old thing, is she? So I added –" she swings a cloak around her shoulders " – sequins!"

The cloak is not very black. It's covered in gold and silver spangly bits. It looks like it should be hanging off a Christmas tree.

"Hmm. I wonder what Mrs Harris will have to say about that?" Zuzanna says.

"I don't care what Mrs Harris says," Chloe says. "She's only the Production Assistant. I deal with the Director, directly. Mrs Lovetofts will love it."

"Mrs Lovetofts loves everything."

"Exactly. Oh yes, and there's one more bit. I forgot."

Chloe sticks her hand into her bag and pulls out a golden crown. It's still cardboard, like the old one, but it

170

has jewels studded all over and sparkling crystal droplets hanging from the top.

"Ta-da!" she says. "Blinging, or what?"

"Wow! Now that is really something," Zuzanna says. "You must have spent ages making that."

"Not me," Chloe says. "My mum. She was up all night. Still, I'm worth it."

"It's brilliant," I say.

"Yes. I'll show Bianca Digby-Cooke who's the best queen."

"Really, Chloe," Zuzanna says, "you shouldn't be so mean about Bianca. She seems like such a nice girl."

"Yes," I say quickly. "She said I made a brilliant rock."

"That's not an actual compliment, Emily," Chloe says.

"Well, some people think being a rock is an extremely difficult role. Somehow you have to get the audience to believe in your character without words or," I pause and look at Chloe's robe, in what I hope is a meaningful way, "elaborate costumes."

Chloe frowns. "A rock doesn't have a character. It's a ... a ... well, it's just a lump."

"Which is why it's such a demanding role," I say. "Not just anyone could do it. It takes a special skill to play a lump. You need to have a sort of ... inner stillness. Mrs Harris obviously thought I was the one who could do it."

"*Inner stillness*? I can do inner stillness. I can do outer stillness as well, I can do all over stillness standing on one leg on tiptoes if necessary!"

"Prove it then. Swap roles," I say. "I'll be the queen and you show how skilfully you can be a rock."

Chloe takes a breath to speak and just for a moment I'm sure she is going to go for it. Then she shrieks, "OMG. What is that?"

I look to where she's pointing. "It's my new rock costume," I say.

"It looks like a box ... with lumps stuck on."

"Told her that already," Zuzanna says.

"They're not lumps, they're rocky premonitions," I say, "or prominations, or protruberations or something – they're to make it look more rocky."

"It looks like it's got a disease!" Chloe says. She swooshes her golden robe around her shoulders again. "No, Emily, a rock is definitely more your sort of thing. Grey is just not my colour. Now, where's my enforcer, Amy-Lee? We need to check up on a few things," she says and walks off, royally.

Zuzanna looks at me and shrugs. "Nice try, Emily, but Chloe was never going to be a rock."

I know it's true. Plan B was a totally rubbish plan. It's just that I've run out of ideas. My creativityness has completely cleared off. I am utterly plan-less.

After ten minutes checking up on everyone

Chloe comes back looking very pleased. Amy-Lee has sloped off to her table, looking a bit disappointed.

"Well, that's all sorted out," Chloe says. "I can report that Phase One of Operation Drama-rama has been a complete success. Everyone seems to have worked very hard on their lines and err ... costumes," Chloe says, pulling a face at my rock box. "Of course we haven't seen the country dancing yet, but so far there has been no need for Amy-Lee to give out any penalties."

"Thank goodness for that," Zuzanna says. "You really shouldn't encourage her, Chloe."

"I'm just using the natural talents of my team," Chloe says.

"What team? You're not actually in charge of this play, Chloe. Mrs Lovetofts and Mrs Harris are."

"Yes, and look where that's got us. Good thing I have impressive leadership skills."

"Well, I'm not sure about your methods,"

Zuzanna says, "but I'd say things are looking up for *The Lost Crown*."

"Urrgh! That title – so dull," Chloe says. "Who wants to come and watch something called *The Lost Crown*? You could fall asleep before you've finished saying it ... We so need a better title. Something more funky and modern."

I have a feeling I'm going to regret asking but I say, "Like what?"

"Oh I don't know, just off the top of my head something like *Whoah Dude! Find My Crown* or *Yo! Bro – My Crown Has Gone to Town*."

"You can't call a play that!" Zuzanna says.

Chloe sighs. "OK, OK. I haven't got time to work on that now anyway, but keep it in mind."

After registration we set off for the Shoestring Theatre again. Lena comes with us. Mrs Lovetofts was very pleased with her scenery and has persuaded Mrs Ahmed to let her be our Assistant Stage Manager's Assistant. Chloe carries her new costume, Lena carries the scenery and I have to carry my rock box without a bin bag now. It's very embarrassing, as everyone we pass stops to have a good stare.

"What's that you've got, dear?" an old lady says as I walk past. "Is it an elephant?"

"No, it's a rock," I say.

"Are you sure? It looks like an elephant." She tilts her head to one side. "With a skin complaint," she says, thoughtfully.

Great. I ask Wavey Cat to give Chloe a mystery virus: first of all he gives one to me, and now he gives one to my costume.

CHAPTER 12

You'll Go Down In History

Shoestring Theatre

At the theatre, I have a lot of trouble getting into the dressing room. The rock has far too many corners. Then I have to try to put it on. You might think it's easy, putting a box over your head, but it's more difficult than it looks.

"For goodness' sake, Emily," Zuzanna says, squeezing past me to get to her chair. "Be more careful with that thing. I'm trying to concentrate. You nearly made me lose my place in the script."

"But you're not reading a script," I say.

"I'm reading it in my head," Zuzanna says.

"I'm sorry, but I can't really see where I'm going," I say, peering out at her through the little hole.

"I'm over here, Emily. You're talking to a coat stand," Zuzanna says. "Why couldn't you have been something more . . . more sensible?"

"It's not my fault Mrs Harris chose me as a rock," I say.

"I thought you said it was because you were a skilled actor." Chloe laughs.

I sigh. "Actually, I think she just doesn't like me."

"Well what do you expect if you assault people with frozen food products?" Chloe says. "Look, can you just go and stand in the corridor for a minute? You are invading my personal space. Totally."

I waddle towards the door, or at least where I *think* the door is.

"Well, go on then," Chloe says.

"Umm . . . could someone open the door for me?" I say.

Unfortunately, just at that moment the door swings open and Elaine yells, "On stage in three minutes, Juniper Road!"

It is very embarrassing to be lying on your back in a cardboard box, with your feet sticking out of the bottom, especially when it is impossible to get up again.

"Ooops, sorry, person in box," Elaine says. "Umm . . . why is there a person in a box?"

"It's Emily," I say "It's my rock costume."

"Oh, right. Of course," Elaine says. "Well, are you all right in there?"

"I think so," I say. I can't feel any bumps or bruises, then again I can't feel anything much because my arms are pinned to my sides.

179

Elaine helps me to stand up and pulls the box off my head. "This costume is a health and safety disaster," she says. "We'll have to keep it up in the wings. Don't put it on until just before you get on stage."

Elaine helps me carry my costume up to the side of the stage. Lena is already there with Mrs Harris, hanging up the scenery at the back. "That looks excellent, Lena," Mrs Harris says, stepping back to admire the eerie forest scene. "I must say you do creepy very well."

"Thank you," Lena says, proudly. "It's my speciality."

"Right, if everyone's ready," Mrs Harris calls, "we'll start another *so-called* rehearsal." She shakes her head sadly. "Quiet on stage, please."

Elaine picks up my rock box and plonks it over my head again.

"Just try not to do anything except stand still," she says in a worried tone.

I would like to explain that standing still is actually the main requirement of a rock but she's already gone.

"And cue music," Mrs Lovetofts says.

There is a lot of quiet.

"Umm. Who is in charge of sound effects?" Mrs Lovetofts asks.

"It was meant to be you, Mrs Lovetofts," Mrs Harris sighs.

"Oh, really?" giggles Mrs Lovetofts. "What a silly I am."

"Shall I do it?" Lena says. "I'm quite good at that sort of thing."

"Thank you, Lena," Mrs Harris says. "You are rapidly becoming indispensable."

Lena beams and sits behind the sound desk.

"ROCKS," Mrs Harris yells and I take a deep breath and waddle out on to the stage. Gross-Out Gavin has also got a rock costume. His is just a sort of grey sack. It is much more practical – at least he can walk. Why are my parents always working out the worst possible way of doing things? I go to find my place at the back of the stage and try to make like a big stony thing and not an elephant with a disease.

Chloe comes on to the stage in her sparkly black cloak. I have to admit she's right, the sequins are a good look. I wait for Mrs Harris to start stressing about it but she doesn't say anything. Perhaps she's got stage exhaustion.

Zuzanna reads the opening lines from the side of the stage. Chloe looks out into the auditorium and says in a clear voice, "Oh dear, why am I wandering about in this forest? I've lost my memory."

She totally doesn't say *totally*. I can't see Mrs Harris from here but I bet she's smiling.

Amy-Lee comes on and does her very convincing witch's cackle and taps Chloe on the arm lightly, then Chloe finishes the scene without one mistake. It's all going very well. It's almost like it's not our play at all.

As the scene ends all the townsfolk pile on to do the country dancing bit. No one trips over, nobody mixes up their do-si-dos with their swing-throughs, nobody's trousers split and the scenery stays in the right place. At the end of the dance, Gross-Out and I have to do our "rocks opening and closing" thing again while all the dancers pile off stage. It is a bit difficult in my box, but I don't bump into anything or fall over. I may finally be getting the hang of being a piece of scenery.

The second half goes really well too, and by the end even Mrs Harris is looking a little happier.

Mrs Lovetofts claps for rather too long then says, "That was much better. Love the cloak, Chloe."

"Thanks," Chloe says, swishing her cloak like a catwalk model. "I think it's more me."

"Tea up!" Elaine calls, clattering in with her trolley.

"You know what," Mrs Harris says, "I might just have one."

Which I think is a very good sign.

Back at school in the afternoon, everyone is totally cheerful.

"I can't believe the country dancers did a whole routine without anyone falling off the stage," Zuzanna says.

"And Operation Drama-rama Phase Two hasn't even started yet," Chloe says.

"What's Phase Two?" I say, feeling a bit worried.

"I don't know, I haven't thought of it yet," Chloe says. "But it definitely involves getting a grand finale. It's the only bit that lets us down now."

"Yes," Zuzanna says. "Mag Hall's is rather polished."

"Well anything they can polish, we can polish, polishier!" Chloe says.

"We can't compete with all those dancing flowers and a chorus of angels, can we?" I say.

"Surely we can come up with something," Chloe says. "I thought you were meant to be creative, Emily."

"I've been having a bit of trouble with that."

"Bianca's toy puppy in the Mag Hall finale is a really cute idea. Maybe we should get a cuddly animal?" Zuzanna says.

"Brilliant!" Chloe says. "I didn't know you had an imagination, Zuzanna."

"A cuddly animal?" I say. "How is that imaginative?"

"Not any old animal – Rudolph!" Chloe says. "I can make my final entrance with my golden robe and crown and Rudolph the Red-Nosed Reindeer.

185

Everyone loves Rudolph! Much better than a stupid toy puppy."

"But where are we going to get a toy reindeer?" I say.

"Not a toy reindeer. That's too much like Mag Hall. How about *someone dressed up as a reindeer*?" Chloe beams.

"But who?" I say.

"You, Emily!"

"Me?!"

"Yes, you. No one will notice if you slip out of your rock box – you can leave it at the back of the stage at the end—"

"But—"

"– and you can wear antlers and a red nose. It'll be perfect."

"But I don't want to be a reindeer!"

"You didn't want to be a rock, either, Emily. It seems a bit like you aren't really backing this play. I thought you wanted a starring role?"

"I do – but that's not a starring role."

"Of course it is – you'll be centre stage in the grand finale!"

"Yes – dressed as Rudolph the Red-Nosed Reindeer. I wanted to be a queen or something!"

"Emily, your acting talents have been very challenged just playing a rock. You should be pleased you are getting this opportunity."

"But the teachers will never agree to it," Zuzanna says. "Will they?"

"Hang on, *I* haven't agreed to it either," I say.

"I think they might," Chloe says, ignoring me. "After all, it's pretty obvious we've got to do some sort of grand finale – just singing a song, especially *that* song, isn't going to help us win."

"I am not being Rudolph!" I say.

"Rudolph?" says Mrs Lovetofts who, with typical teacher terrible timing, has just walked in to class.

"Yes," Chloe says and quickly explains her new idea, adding, "No one will notice if Emily slips out of her rock box at the end, and Emily so wanted a role with moving parts."

"Do you know, I think that's rather good," giggles Mrs Lovetofts. "I was very impressed with the cast today and Lena's scenery is marvellous, but I must say the play lacks a certain sparkle at the end. Rudolph might be just what we need! I'll have a word with Mrs Harris. And well done – that's a very good idea, Emily." She goes off humming "Rudolph the Red-Nosed Reindeer".

I cannot believe this has happened. Why did I have to wish for a starring role? If I have to be Rudolph, how am I going to tell Bella that I was ill? I will be right in the middle of the stage with a red nose! She won't need to come to the play because she will probably be able to see me from Wales! I stomp all the way home and slam the front door. "Wavey Cat – you never do wishes properly!" I say and I stuff him behind a cushion.

CHAPTER 13

Bully For Who?

Thursday afternoon

It's our last but one rehearsal. We did two on Tuesday, two yesterday and one this morning, all with no disasters. Tomorrow we get one more run through and then we do the play for real. In front of a whole room full of audience – and Bella. Everyone is nervous but excited. Chloe, Zuzanna and I are in our dressing room, waiting for Elaine to call us to go up to the stage. Now that my box is being kept upstairs there is room for us all to fit in together again, although Chloe still wants all the mirror to herself.

"I don't see why you need to look in the mirror," she says, barging me out of the way with her elbow. "It doesn't matter what you look like, no one's going to see you in your box, are they?"

"Well, yes. They are now, actually. Now that you've arranged for me to be Rudolph," I say, trying to see past her.

"Emily, Rudolph is a reindeer. The audience will not expect to see a glamorous reindeer."

"I'm not trying to make myself look glamorous," I say. "I'm trying to get this red nose to stay on." Mrs Lovetofts supplied me with a red nose and a pair of cardboard antlers this morning. It is obviously a red

nose left over from Red Nose
Day. I'm trying not to think about who
else's nose might have once been inside it. I have
tried to disguise myself by pulling my hair back
in a tight ponytail and wearing an expression of
reindeer-ish thoughtfulness. But I am definitely
recognisably Emily Sparkes – Bella will know
straight away.

Over the last couple of days, I've spent ages
trying to think of an excuse to explain to Bella why
I am a reindeer, not royalty.

I thought I'd say:

"I couldn't play the queen because I was too
ill but then I had a minor medical miracle and
felt better, but by then it was too late and Chloe
was already playing the queen, but then the
person who was going to play Rudolph got ill
and so I decided to be Rudolph to save the day."

Then I realised that's so complicated I'm
bound to mess it up and anyway it sounds

about as convincing as Chloe's latest story about turning down a Hollywood movie because there were too many vegetables on the lunch menu.

I am just going to have to confess that I lied and Bella is going to think not only am I a rubbish actor but I am also not really a very good friend and that she is better off with New Emily after all, which is probably true, to be honest.

The rehearsal has gone very well, again. Lena has come up with some creepy new sound effects for the forest scene and she even brought in Barney, her stuffed crow, to sit in a tree. Even my Rudolph bit is a big success, when I was really hoping it would be a disaster. I have to crawl in on all fours with

Chloe walking beside me in her crown and robe. I was trying to keep my head down but then Mrs Harris said she wanted us all to stand at the front for the final song so here I am, centre stage, with a big red nose and antlers.

"Wonderful!" calls Mrs Lovetofts. "Very well done. Emily, you're a natural as a reindeer. Now, back to the dressing rooms, everyone. Chloe, your mum is outside, waiting to take you to your dentist's appointment."

"Do you have toothache?" I ask hopefully. Perhaps there's still time – maybe my luck is about to have a tooth-related turnaround. Chloe frowns at me. "No, Emily, it's just a check-up."

I have reached the bottom of the barrel of hope, there is no more luck left in my bucket. Fortune has fantastically frowned on me. I have to accept that Chloe is going to be the queen and I'm going to be ... an embarrassment. No, worse than that, a dishonest embarrassment – wearing antlers.

"Quick as you can please, Chloe," Mrs Lovetofts calls. "Apparently you're running late."

"You can't hurry royalty," Chloe says. "Really, the dentist should come to me."

I follow her and Zuzanna down the stairs back to the dressing room.

"Hold on," Lena calls, catching us up. "How do you think today's rehearsal went? How were the sound effects?"

"Yes, very good," Chloe says, "although I could have done without that giant eagle thing staring at me the whole time."

"He's a crow," Lena says. "He's really pretty friendly." She grins. "Are you walking home, Emily?"

"Yes, just need to get my things," I say.

There's a light laugh and
we walk in to find Bianca
already standing in front of the
mirror, pinning up her hair. Willow is
standing next to her, holding hair clips and
passing them to her whenever she says "*Now.*"
Lavender is sitting in a chair, chewing her plait and
looking bored.

"Hello, girls," Bianca says. "How was it today?"

"Much better, thanks," Zuzanna says. "We seem
to be getting the hang of it at last."

"Really?" Bianca says. "I noticed your new
scenery. It's very good."

"Lena made it," I say.

"Hi," Lena says.

Bianca looks her up and down and raises one
eyebrow (which is quite a cool thing to do, I might
practise). "What unusual shoes," she says, looking
at the big, black, clumpy shoes Lena loves to wear.
"Yes. I can tell you're the arty type."

195

Lena looks at her but doesn't smile, although that's not unusual for Lena.

"We've got some new costumes, too," Zuzanna says. "Chloe's got a great robe and crown now."

"So I see," Bianca says. "You really have made an effort!" she laughs.

Chloe dumps her cloak and crown on the chair and grabs her bag. "See you later," she says, and dashes out again.

"Oh, dear. Chloe always seems so cross with me," Bianca says.

"She's probably just worried about the dentist," I say, trying to cover up for her.

"It's nice that Chloe has got you as friends," Bianca says. "Like a fresh start. *Now*, Willow."

Willow quickly hands her a hair clip.

"What do you mean by 'a fresh start'?" Zuzanna says.

"Oh, you know. New school. New friends. It's good to know she's got over her . . . issues."

 I don't know what issues Bianca means. Chloe has tons of issues, mostly to do with thinking she's more important than anyone else, and I've never noticed her getting over any of them.

"Look, what *is* all this thing with Chloe? Why did she leave Mag Hall anyway?" Zuzanna says.

"I don't really want to – I mean, it was a while ago now." Bianca looks a little upset now.

"But what happened?" Zuzanna insists. "And why doesn't anyone want to talk about it?"

"We just had a few ... bullying issues."

"Bullying! You don't mean Chloe was actually bullying someone?"

"You know, she can be a bit ... well, she likes people to do things her way. *Now*, Willow."

"I guess she can be a bit bossy," I say, "but not in a really bad way."

"You see, she came to our school when her mum

got a job there. As a cleaner," Bianca says. "Thing is, she never really seemed to like me. Did she, Lavender?"

Lavender shakes her head and spits out her plait. "No. That's true," she says.

"Things really got bad when she wanted the lead in the school play – but, of course, I got it," Bianca says. "She was very annoyed. She told me I should give her the part because she would do a better job."

"That does sound like Chloe, but it's not really bullying, is it?" I say.

"But then I noticed some of the younger girls were a bit nervous of her, too. It started off with her just being bossy. You know the sort of thing, making them carry her bags, getting them to hold the door open for her. It all got a bit out of hand when she started making them hand over their sweets and chocolate."

Zuzanna gasps, "No!"

"But I can't imagine Chloe being like that," I say. Or can I? I'm starting to feel a bit confused. I look over at Lena. She hasn't joined in the conversation, but I can't read her expression.

"I don't think she had a lot of money, you see – you know, with her mum being just a *cleaner* – so she was a bit envious of some of the girls who do. *Now*, Willow," Bianca says, and gets another hair clip.

"But that's awful," Zuzanna says. "What happened?"

"I didn't want to get her into trouble," Bianca says. "But I had to tell someone, because it was unfair on the younger kids. She had to leave in the end. Her mother lost her job too."

Zuzanna gasps again. "Terrible."

"You won't say anything, will you?" Bianca says. "It's all in the past now. I've tried to be friendly

towards her but she still obviously doesn't like me. I ... I wouldn't want it to all start up again."

"What start up again?" Zuzanna says.

"The ... nasty texts. I've changed my number, but I'm still worried."

"No! That's awful," Zuzanna says. "That's ... cyber-bullying!"

Bianca gives her a weak smile. "Thanks for the support, girls. Come on, Lavender. Hurry up, Willow! Time for our rehearsal. Bring the puppy and my crown."

"I knew it!" Zuzanna says when they've left. "I knew there was something going on. Why else would Chloe keep trying to avoid Bianca? She was scared she was going to say something."

"But I can't believe it," I say. "Chloe wouldn't bully little kids."

"But she does do things like make people carry

her bag and pull out her chair, doesn't she?" Zuzanna says. "It's only a short step from being bossy to bullying. Look how friendly she's been getting with Amy-Lee."

"But sending nasty texts?"

"She's always texting, though, isn't she? Imagine if you'd upset her – she'd definitely have something to say. What if she starts cyber-bullying us?" She gives a little shudder.

I'm feeling very uncomfortable about this. Zuzanna, however, seems convinced.

"I wondered why she was so offish with Bianca all the time. Obviously, she's still mad at her for reporting the bullying. All this time I thought she was making Mag Hall up, otherwise why didn't she go back there? Well, now we know. She's been excluded!"

When Zuzanna says "She's been excluded" it sounds as if she's saying "She's been sentenced to ten years in prison."

Zuzanna is going to her granny's so Lena and I walk home together.

"All that stuff about Chloe. I can hardly believe it," I say. "She's never been like that to us. I know she's pretty bossy, but I don't think she'd steal. Although there was that time she took the pack of card from outside the secretary's office but she did put it back, although only when someone found out. Do you think she's a bully?" I look at Lena but she is looking at the ground with her hands shoved in her pockets. I realise that I have been chattering on but she has hardly spoken. In fact she hasn't really said much since we went into the dressing room. "Is everything all right, Lena?" I ask.

"What? Oh. Yeah, I'm OK," she says.

"Are you sure? You've gone really quiet."

"It just brought back some memories."

"What did?"

"Listening to that Bianca."

"Memories? Oh, no! I forgot – you were bullied in your last school, weren't you? And I've been going on and on. I'm really sorry. Are you sure you're OK?"

She smiles. "Yes, I'm fine. It just got me thinking. Anyway, I've got a new school now, haven't I? I've made a fresh start."

"Yes, definitely. You're not getting bullied here."

"And so has Chloe, so maybe we should give her a chance, too," Lena says. "After all, we don't *really* know what went on, do we?"

"Well, Bianca was pretty clear about it."

"Yeah. I know," Lena says.

CHAPTER 14

Excuse Me, Could I Borrow Your Reindeer?

Friday morning

Today I am mostly feeling faint. I am feeling faint with excitement and also faint with worry, so I'm not really sure which faint I am feeling at any one time. I am excited because we will be performing in a theatre tonight and also because I get to see Bella this afternoon. But I am completely worried

205

because I don't know how I'm going to tell Bella the truth – she will think I'm a completely big, pants-on-fire liar and give up being my best friend totally.

I am also very confused about Chloe. Zuzanna has hardly spoken to her all morning, although I don't think Chloe's really noticed that much, as she's been practising her lines and working on being royal, which is mostly bossing people around as usual.

We arrive a little early at the theatre and Mag Hall are still doing their last rehearsal.

"Oooh good, we get to sit and watch their lovely play again," says Mrs Lovetofts.

We all walk quietly into the auditorium and find a seat, just in time for the grand finale.

The music begins and all the littlees come on stage. They do look really pretty in their flower costumes. They do some twirly dancing and then Edwina and Lavender do the chorus of angels bit. Finally, Bianca comes on with Willow cheerfully carrying her train and, I can't believe it, Bianca's holding a real puppy!

It's so cute it looks as though it's just having a day off from advertising toilet roll. Bianca sings her solo and brings the puppy to the front of the stage for a final bow.

Mrs Lovetofts claps like she has just seen a smash-hit West End musical. "Wonderful, Mr Garrick," she says. "A real puppy – what a lovely idea!"

Chloe huffs loudly. "That's so much better than a girl dressed as a reindeer. If there's one thing an audience likes it's a puppy. We may as well give up now." And she gets up and walks out. Zuzanna and I follow her to where she is sitting in reception.

"We changed the costumes, the dancing, we even learned our lines – and now Bianca Digby-Cooke goes and outsmarts us with a puppy!" Chloe says.

"It's not a competition, Chloe," Zuzanna snaps.

"We wanted to get better so we wouldn't let our school down, and we have got better. That's all that matters."

"Bianca's bound to win the Best Young Actor Award," Chloe says, ignoring her.

"So? If you ask me you're letting this thing with Bianca get out of hand!" Zuzanna says. I don't think I've ever seen her so cross – well, not since I accidentally spilled blackcurrant squash on her new white socks. "Look, Chloe," she says, "we know why you left Mag Hall. Bianca told us all about the bullying."

Chloe gasps. "Really? She told you?"

"Yes, she did," Zuzanna says. "So, you're not even going to deny it?"

"I just don't want to talk about it, OK? I came to this school to make a fresh start and get away from all that – and now Mag Hall turn up here."

Zuzanna does a cross sigh and folds her arms

in a "not impressed" kind of way, and then they both lapse into a sulky silence.

"Look," I say brightly, trying to cheer things up, "let's concentrate on the play and do our best for the school and Mrs Lovetofts. I know puppies are cute," I add, thinking on my feet, "but what if we had an animal too ... like a reindeer!"

"We have got a reindeer, Emily. That's what you're supposed to be! What did you think you were, a horse with a couple of twigs on its head?" Chloe's moment of sulky silence seems to have passed quite quickly.

"We could put a bow on her antlers," Zuzanna says, looking at me thoughtfully. Then she shakes her head. "No, it's going to take a lot more than that to make Emily cute."

"But what if we had a baby reindeer, a real one?" I say. I am not sure where this idea has come from, I may have actually gone a little crazy with school-play fever, but I am also slightly thinking, *What if we could get a real reindeer?* Then at least I wouldn't have to come on as one, and Bella wouldn't see me.

"Emily, that might be the most stupid idea you've ever had, and that makes it very stupid indeed," Chloe says. "Where on earth do you think we are going to find a real reindeer?"

"Well, perhaps we could phone the zoo or, I don't know, find a person from Finland with a pet we could borrow."

"Look Emily, I know you're trying to be helpful but Mag Hall have got voice coaching and drama lessons and script-writers and ballet classes and costume designers *and a real, live puppy!*"

"Well, we've got one thing they haven't," I say proudly.

"What's that?" Zuzanna asks.

"Emily Sparkes creativityness!" I say, and I really hope it's true.

I go to find Lena to see if she wants to walk home, but she's doing last-minute scenery repairs.

"I don't know how this keeps happening," she says. "There's a big hole poked through the wall of the castle. And a couple of days ago there was quite a nasty rip in the forest."

"You don't know anyone with a baby reindeer, do you?" I say.

"Err ... No. Why?"

"I just need a cute animal."

"You could borrow Barney," she says brightly.

"Thanks," I say, "but I was looking for something a little less ... stuffed."

When I get home Mum and Gran are in the kitchen.

"Do you know any Nordic people, Mum?" I ask.

"I don't think so. There's a lady at the library from Ipswich, though."

"Ipswich?"

"Yes, that's not far from Norwich."

"*Nordic*, Mum. You know – like Finland, Sweden, Iceland."

"Mrs Wooley down the road spends a lot of time in Iceland," Gran says.

"Really?" I say. "She doesn't have a reindeer, does she?"

"I don't think so. But she swears by their frozen prawns."

"You mean the shop, don't you, Gran," I say with a sigh.

I look up the number for the zoo. The lady who answers the phone is very nice but she says they mostly have animals from Africa and Asia, plus a few penguins. Just out of interest I ask her if they ever employ camel whisperers, but she doesn't seem to know what I mean.

The girls were right. The baby reindeer plan was completely stupid. I am just grasping at desperate ideas because I don't want Bella to see me in a Rudolph costume. My creativityness has gone. I have lost it all by telling lies. I am no longer Emily Sparkes, creative genius, I am just plain old Emily Sparkes – mainly girl, occasionally reindeer.

"Cheer up," Mum says, walking in and actually noticing I'm fed up for once. "I've got a surprise for you. Bella's mum phoned. They're a bit earlier than they thought they'd be so they're going to pop in for a bit, before going to Auntie Penny's. They should be here in about half an hour."

CHAPTER 15

Ciao, Bella!

Friday afternoon

I am waiting for Bella to arrive. She can only stay for an hour because she has to see her auntie and cousins, too. Then she's coming to the play this evening. I have decided to be brave. I am not going to do any more lying or pretending to be ill. I am going to tell her the truth. I will say that I made the whole queen thing up and I'm sorry. I just have to wait for the right moment.

Now it's nearly time for her to arrive I feel a bit strange – like I need to polish a bit of myself or something. I know she won't mind what I look like or anything, but I can't help feeling a bit nervous. I've tidied up my room and it looks really good now. Bella won't believe it. Last time she saw it, it was grubby pink with a teddy painted on the wall. I'm very glad my mum redecorated it recently. It took me ages to find Wavey Cat, though. I forgot I'd stuffed him under a cushion. Luckily he doesn't seem too bothered about it and he's still smiling and waving. I have put him in pride of place in the middle of my dressing table.

The doorbell goes at exactly four thirty. It's not like Bella to be on time – I hope nothing else about her has changed. I should race to answer the door but suddenly I have butterflies about seeing her again. What if she looks totally different? What if we can't find anything to talk about? I don't really know much about goats, especially Welsh ones.

"Emily, Bella's here," Mum calls.

I go downstairs and there, in the middle of the living room, is Bella – real Bella!

"Wahhhhh!" she says and rushes at me to give me a hug and then everything is fine and normal and Bella is just the same and it's OK.

"Come and see my new room," I say.

"Aren't you going to say hello to Bella's mum?" my mum says.

"Hello, Mrs Adams," I call over my shoulder.

Mum laughs and they go off to natter and drink tea.

"Wow, this room is amazing!" Bella says. "You're so lucky – mine's still the way it was when it was the last owner's spare room, and I think they must have used their spare room for storing goat food."

{ 217 }

"Your hair's grown," I say. Bella's always had quite short hair but now it's longer and more curly.

"Yes, I'm thinking of growing it," she says. "Emily's – I mean *New* Emily's – hair is really long and she does lots of things with braids and stuff, it's cool."

Bella used to hate braids and hair things, and now I come to look at her closely I think she might be wearing eyeliner. I think I must be staring at her a bit too hard because she suddenly jumps up and starts looking around my room.

"Hey look – it's Wavey Cat," Bella says, flicking his paw.

"I'm always asking him to bring you back," I say, "but he never does."

"Well, I'm here now," Bella says. "Can't wait to see you in the show tonight. Can you remember all your lines?"

"Err ... yes," I say, which is not an actual lie. "How's school?"

We talk about her school and my school and how different it is for her living in the countryside and we even talk a bit about goats. I keep waiting for the right moment to tell her I'm not the queen but it doesn't seem to come.

"Emily," Mum calls up the stairs after what seems like five minutes but is nearly an hour. "Bella's got to go in a minute."

"Oh, no!" I say.

"Sorry – Auntie Penny is cooking a special tea, but I'll see you at the play tonight. Can't wait!" Bella says.

"I know," I say, taking a deep breath. "I wanted to tell you something about that."

"What?"

"You know I said I'm playing the queen?"

"Yes, it's so cool. I was telling New Emily all

about it the other day. I think she's a bit jealous, to be honest!"

"Really?" I say, weakly.

"Emily!" Mum calls. "You girls need to come down now."

"Come down to the van," Bella says. "I've got something to show you."

I follow her downstairs and out on to the front drive. "Look," Bella says, pointing into the back of the small van with "Adams' Goat's Cheese" written down the side.

I peer through the back window and see, snuggled up on a bed of straw, a goat! A little, tiny goat.

"It's Clover," Bella says. "She gets sad if I leave her behind – I don't think she realises she's not a human."

We climb in the back of the van. Clover is very tame, she sort of curls up next to Bella and eats some hay.

"I don't think you'd really want to come back now, would you?" I say.

Bella looks away. "I miss it, I miss school and you and stuff but ... if I came back I'd miss Clover and pony trekking and New Emily – so, I don't know any more."

I feel like a sort of heavy thing has got stuck in my chest.

"I do wish you could come back," I say, "but I also want you to be happy."

"You've got new friends, too, though," Bella says. "Zuzanna and Chloe. If I hadn't gone to Wales you wouldn't have been friends with them."

"It's not the same, though," I say. "They're not my first-best friends."

Bella smiles. "Don't worry, we'll always be first-best friends. Even if we move to Australia to make kangaroo cheese!"

Bella's mum opens the van door. "Ah, there you are! We should've guessed. Time to go now, I'm sorry. Auntie Penny will have our tea ready."

We clamber out of the van.

"Say goodbye to Clover, Emily," Bella says.

"Clover?" Mum says.

I slam the van door quickly before Mum realises she's accidentally named her baby after a small, slightly smelly farm animal. Bella climbs into the front seat.

"See you tonight, Your Majesty," she laughs.

I watch them as they drive away and I don't feel like anyone's best friend.

At the theatre everyone is in a state of total nervousness-ish-ness. Chloe is in the corridor, walking up and down doing her Darth Vader breathing. Zuzanna and I are in the dressing room. Zuzanna is reading her script again even though she knows it so well she could probably do it backwards (although that really *would* mess up the play). Even the Mag Hall girls are looking a bit apprehensive as they finish their make-up. At least their play is first up, so we get a bit of time to ourselves to prepare.

I can't believe I didn't tell Bella the truth. It just never seemed to be the right time. Or, what I really mean is, I just wasn't brave enough.

Elaine sticks her head around the door. "The audience is in," she says. "Mag Hall – time to head for the stage, please. Good luck, everyone!"

"Good luck, Juniper Road," Bianca says as they walk out. "Break a leg, Chloe," she adds as they pass in the corridor.

As soon as the Mag Hall girls leave, Chloe slips back into the room. "Thank goodness that lot have gone," she says. "They totally hog the mirror."

"So how did you get on finding a baby reindeer, Emily?" Zuzanna says. "Are you having one flown in from Finland by special delivery?"

"Probably got Father Christmas on the case, right now," Chloe adds, and they both burst into giggles. It seems they've managed to find something to bond over again.

"At least I tried," I say.

"Don't worry, Emily, your Rudolph will be fine," Zuzanna says.

"I suppose I was being a bit negative," Chloe says. "Put it down to actor burnout. Now I totally need my hairbrush." Chloe rummages through the bag hanging on her chair. "Hang on," she says, "where is my golden robe? And my new crown, come to that?"

"They must be there somewhere," Zuzanna says, strolling over to help her look. "Probably under all these make-up bags," she adds disapprovingly.

"They're not here," Chloe says, with a hint of

panic in her voice. I go to help with the search. We look through all of our bags and costumes but there's no sign of Chloe's crown or her golden robe.

"Are you sure you didn't take them home?" Zuzanna says.

"No, of course not. I left everything here earlier, after this morning's rehearsal. Someone must have moved them," she says, looking over to where the Mag Hall girls have left their bags hanging on the back of their chairs. Chloe marches purposefully over to Bianca's bag and starts looking through it.

"Chloe! You can't go through other people's things, it's ... it's illegal," I say.

"Well you'd better stand in front of the door and stop anyone coming in then," she says.

"I am having nothing to do with this," Zuzanna says and does her foldy-arm thing again and looks the other way.

I lean against the door and will Chloe to hurry up. She moves from Bianca's bag to Lavender's and

soon she has gone through all the Mag Hall girls'
things, but there is definitely no crown or robe to
be found.

"Nothing," Chloe says.

"Well, what did you expect?" Zuzanna says. "It's
not as if they would have stolen them, is it?"

"Shows what you know," Chloe says.

"But what are we going to do about
your costume?" I say. "It's part of the
grand finale."

"You'll just have to wear this,"
Zuzanna says, holding up the faded pink
towel, "and your old crown. Perhaps we could fix it
with a bit of Sellotape," she adds doubtfully.

"Marvellous," Chloe says. "It just gets better
and better. This isn't going to be a grand finale, it's
going to be a grand fiasco!"

"We've got time," Zuzanna says. "We'll
keep searching. Your costume must be
somewhere. I'll go to look in the wings.

Emily, you check reception, by the seats where we were sitting earlier."

I march off dutifully. I never argue with Zuzanna when she's in organiser mode (which is most of the time, really).

But the costume is not in reception. I look behind the chairs and even ask the lady at the desk but no one has handed in any royal robes lately. I can hear the music start for the beginning of the Mag Hall play. I just can't think where else to look.

I wander out to the car park. Maybe Chloe dropped it on her way home, or it might be stuck in a tree or something.

I am just inspecting the trees when there's a loud "Beeeeeep" from behind me. I spin around to see Bella laughing and waving from the window of her mum's van. The van pulls into a parking space and she jumps down.

"Hah! We made you jump. Sorry, we're a bit late.

Auntie Penny's tea went on for a *really* long time. We haven't missed it, have we?"

"No, no. The first play has only just started. We haven't done ours yet."

"Hadn't you better hurry up and get your queen costume on?" Bella says, looking me up and down. "I'm dying to see what you look like."

"Err, yeah. You might be quite surprised," I say.

We're just going to get Clover out for a minute," Bella says, walking around to the back of the van. "Let her stretch her legs."

"Meeeeeh," Clover says, jumping down into the car park. She flutters her long, goaty eyelashes. You know, she really is a very cute goat.

And then, finally, I get a flash of Emily Sparkes creativityness.

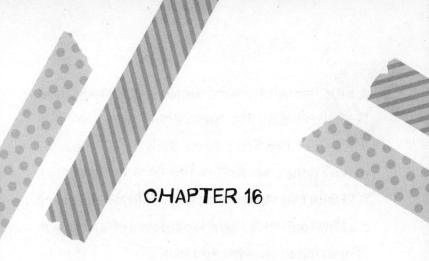

CHAPTER 16

Return of the Creativityness!

Friday night

"Where have you been, Emily?" Zuzanna says as I walk in, she is frowning at least a 4.3.

"Yes!" Chloe says. "You need to get ready – we're on in ten minutes!"

"Eight, actually," Zuzanna says.

Lena is also there. "I've been helping look for the

costume," she says. "But we haven't found it. First the scenery, and now this." She frowns.

"Hurry up, Emily. You need to make sure your reindeer costume is ready," Chloe says.

"There's been a slight change of plan," I say. *A genius change of plan, actually*, I think. A plan in which I don't have to be Rudolph after all.

"A change of plan?! Emily, the show is starting in eight minutes."

"Seven, now," Zuzanna says, unhelpfully.

"I know. I know. Come with me, quickly. I want to show you something."

Lena, Zuzanna and Chloe follow me down the corridor to the back door of the theatre.

"I don't think you're supposed to open that, except in an emergency," Zuzanna says, pointing to a sign which reads, "Do Not Open Except in an Emergency".

"This is an emergency," I say.

"But it might be alarmed!"

Not as alarmed as you're going to be in a minute, I think.

I push down the bar and open the door. Luckily, no bells ring and Bella is standing there just like we arranged.

"Bella!" Zuzanna says.

"Hi girls," Bella says. "Surprise!"

"You're supposed to be in Wales," Zuzanna says, as if Bella's broken a rule. She's not that keen on surprises. "And ... what's *that*?" Her eyes open wide at the sight of Clover, who is peeping up at her from behind Bella's legs.

"You will look after her, won't you?" Bella says to me. "She can get a bit ... overexcited."

"Don't worry, she'll be fine," I say, taking Clover by the lead that Bella has attached to her collar. "She's going to be a star!"

"A star?" Chloe says. "Oh no. Please tell me I've got this wrong."

"Good luck," Bella says. "Got to get to my seat."

"Oh yes, and actually, did I mention I don't feel very well?" I call after her but she's already gone.

"A goat!" Chloe says as I close the door again. "Please don't tell me you expect me to act with a goat."

"Mehhhhhhh," Clover says, and sniffs Chloe's feet.

"You just need to use your imagination, Chloe. Think of it as a baby reindeer," I say. "We just have to put the false antlers and red nose on her – no one will know the difference."

"*I* will know," Chloe wails. "I can't act with a goat!"

"Of course you can, Chloe. An actor of your talent can act with anything. And we needed something spectacular for the grand finale, right?" I say.

"But a goat isn't spectacular … it's, it's all goaty."

"She will look super-spectacular when we dress her up. Come on, Chloe, I know you can do it," I say. Finally, my Emily Sparkes creativityness has come to the rescue. I don't have to be centre stage as Rudolph any more. Now, all I have to tell Bella is that I was ill and Chloe had to take my place as queen and she'll never know I lied.

"I think she's cool," Lena says, stroking Clover's back.

"But where are we going to keep her?" Zuzanna says, snatching her hand away as Clover nibbles her fingers.

"In the dressing room, I suppose," I say, although I haven't actually managed to think that through yet.

"All the Mag Halls will be in the dressing room in a minute, we can't leave her with them," Chloe says.

"Look, I had a flash of creativityness. I haven't worked out the finer details."

"What about the boys' dressing room?" Zuzanna says. "We could leave her in there – it'll be empty because everyone will be up waiting in the wings – then you could sneak out and get her just before the grand finale, Emily."

"Good idea," I say.

"I can't believe you're going along with this, Zuzanna," Chloe says.

"I know. Neither can I, really," Zuzanna says. "But we have to do something grand and finale-ish, and you haven't even got a costume at the moment."

Chloe does a dramatic wail but it is drowned out by the sound of loud applause from the auditorium. Mag Hall have finished.

"Juniper Road, you're next," Elaine's voice comes floating down the corridor as she bangs on the boys' dressing room door.

"Quick, you need to hide the goat," Lena says. She opens the door to a cleaning cupboard. "In here!"

I drag Clover, who is not being very co-operative, into the cupboard with me and Lena shuts the door on us. It's completely dark. "It's OK, Clover," I say. "Don't be scared, we'll be out in a minute."

"Meeeeeh," Clover says.

"Shhh, Clover. Someone will hear us."

Clover starts making little munching noises. I can't see what she's eating but at least it's keeping her quiet.

"Hello girls." I hear Elaine's voice through the cupboard door. "What are you doing out here in the corridor? Ready to go on stage?"

"Yes, just coming," Chloe says.

"Good. Ah, here are Bianca and the others. Well done, girls – excellent performance. Loved the puppy," Elaine says.

"Thank you," Bianca says. "I think it went really well."

"Such lovely girls," Elaine says and the Mag Hall girls giggle as they go into the dressing room.

"Hurry up, Juniper Road," Elaine says. "The rest of the cast have gone up already," and she heads back to the stage.

Chloe opens the cupboard door. "Quick," she says, "while there's no one about."

I pull Clover out of the cupboard. She's dragging something out behind her. It's sort of gold and curtain-y ...

"My robe!" Chloe says. "And there's my crown, too!"

"Well done, Clover!" I say, holding the robe up. "Oh."

Clover has taken several large bites out of Chloe's robe and also a big one out of her crown.

"Aaaaaargh!" Chloe says. "Goats are now

236

officially my number one least favourite animal. Reindeer are next."

"Umm ... well at least we've found your costume," I say.

"Oh, dear," says a voice from behind us. "That looks like a bit of a write-off. What a horrible thing to happen to your lovely costume, Chloe."

Bianca is standing in the doorway of the dressing room, looking concerned. "I hate to mention it, but ... you do know there's a goat standing next to you, don't you?"

"Oh yes, so there is," I say, in what I hope is a "How did that get there?" sort of way.

"A goat, a squashed crown and a half-eaten curtain. It's going to be an interesting play." Bianca smiles. "I hope you managed to get your scenery fixed in time."

"How did you know about that?" Lena says sharply.

"Oh, err ... I just pick things up, you know? By the way, aren't you meant to be on stage?"

"Come on," Zuzanna says. "We're late!"

We race up the corridor with Clover and I shove her through the door of the boys' dressing room. "Stay here, Clover," I say. "I'll be back soon." I shut the door and we hurry upstairs.

CHAPTER 17

{ What Could Possibly Go Wrong? }

Showtime!

This is it. I stand in the wings and listen to the chatter of the crowd on the other side of the closed curtain.

"Rocks, get ready to go on," Mrs Harris whispers, as Mrs Lovetofts dumps the box on my head. Gross-Out and I take our places on the stage and the music starts.

I peer out through the little slot at the front of my rock box. The curtains open and I am amazed how many people are filling the auditorium. It's very hard to make out anyone in the audience individually, but I'm almost certain that must be my dad's bald head reflecting the stage lights near the front. I hear a baby shout, "Ehhhhhhhhhhhh," and I smile, knowing my sister is out there supporting me.

The music dies away and Zuzanna reads, "Once there was a queen who was having a bad day."

"Oh dear, why am I wandering about in this forest?" Chloe says, coming on to the stage, and the play is underway.

Twenty minutes in and I can't believe how well it's going. The country dancers have done their thing twice and no one got even slightly maimed. Gavin and I did our clashing rocks and no one fell over. Just the end of this scene in the forest to go,

240

and then it will be time for the grand finale. Oh no, the grand finale – I almost forgot. I need to get Clover.

I wait till the spotlight is directly on Chloe then I creep out from under my box and crawl off through the wings. I am just slipping past the other actors when I hear a funny little clippety-cloppety noise coming up the stairs. I know that sound. But it can't be, she's shut in the dressing room. But it is. Oh, no! Clover! How did she get out?

"Mehhhhh," Clover says and trots straight into the wings as if she was born for the stage.

"What is *that*? Mrs Lovetofts says in a loud whisper, as Clover clip-clops to a halt next to her.

"It's just a pet," I say, making a grab for Clover's lead, which is trailing behind her.

"It's a goat!" she says.

"Yes. It's a goat-shaped pet," I reply.

"Meeeeeeeeeh," Clover says, backing away from me.

241

"Come on, Clover," I say. "Come to Emily."

Clover looks at me with her goaty eyes and stamps her hooves.

"Come on, now. There's a good goat," I say, taking a step closer.

Clover looks at me and then looks at the stage.

"Clover! No!" I yell, making a desperate leap towards her.

"Mehhhhhhhhhhhhhhh!" she bleats and makes a dash for freedom and the open stage.

"Clover, come back!"

The audience roar with laughter as Clover clatters into view and right through the middle of the country dancers' skipping in pairs routine.

She runs around in a big circle and all the dancers squeal and try to jump out of her way. Small Emily B. trips over backwards and lands on top of Alfie Balfour, Alfie bumps into Gracie who knocks into the scenery and then screams as Barney the stuffed crow lands on her. The audience roar with laughter as Clover bolts back across the stage in front of them.

I run on and make a grab for Clover's collar but she's too fast, and clatters off into the wings on the opposite side. I dash across the stage but before I get there she is already running back on again, and she seems to have got a pair of Mag Hall's angel wings stuck on her back. The crowd shriek with laughter as she does five more circuits of the stage before finally coming to a stop and munching on some plastic grass near the front. I grab her collar and drag her off.

The audience is still laughing, even as the villagers try to finish their dance. Well, the villagers who have managed to get back on their feet and are not involved in holding up bits of scenery or comforting a hysterical Gracie.

Just when I think things could not possibly get worse, I see Mrs Harris hurrying up the steps.

"What on earth is going on?" Mrs Harris manages to sound like she's shouting even when she's whispering. "Emily Sparkes! I might have known you'd be behind this."

"She's supposed to be a reindeer," I say, and even I realise that sounds a bit feeble.

"No, Emily. She is a goat!" Mrs Harris says. "In what way did you think a runaway goat would improve this performance?"

I'm not sure I can remember that myself now. "She wasn't supposed to be a runaway. I don't know how she got out."

"And I don't know how she got in," Elaine says, coming up the steps behind Mrs Harris. "There is a very clear no goat policy at the Shoestring Theatre."

"We'll deal with this later," Mrs Harris says. "I think I'd better stay here for now, I've got a play to rescue. And get rid of that … creature!"

"Clover!" Now it's Bella coming up the stairs.

"I told you to hang on tight to her, Emily," she says, taking Clover's lead. "She loves running away."

"Sorry," I say, "perhaps having a goat as a reindeer wasn't a very good idea."

Bella laughs. "She certainly did get a starring role! Almost as much of a star as you, Emily."

"Me?" Surely even Bella can't think that being a runaway-goat catcher counts as a starring role. "Look, about that – it's just that I felt really ill and—"

"Amazing. The show must go on, eh? No one would have known you felt poorly. I honestly didn't recognise you in that black glittery cloak."

"Glittery cloak?"

Bella untangles the angel wings from Clover's lead and hands them to me. "Come on, Clover, we'd better get you back to the van. I'll only be a minute, though. I don't want to miss you in the grand finale, Emily," she calls over her shoulder

totally as she disappears down the stairs with Clover clippity-clopping behind her.

Oh, no. Bella still thinks I'm the queen. I suppose Chloe has had her hood up the whole time and if Bella's sitting near the back, she must have thought it was me in that cloak. She's still expecting to see me come on at the end – in a sparkling crown and robe!

The villagers have recovered enough to finish their dance and come off stage. At least the audience have mostly stopped laughing now.

Mrs Harris says weakly, "Grand finale. Places, everyone."

Chloe growls, "What a disaster. Emily, you're just a walking calamity! Come on, we need to save what's left of this play. Get your antlers *oooooooo-oooooooooooooooooooooon!*" she shrieks, as she slips and lands on her bottom.

"What now?!" Mrs Harris says.

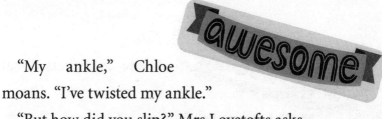

"My ankle," Chloe moans. "I've twisted my ankle."

"But how did you slip?" Mrs Lovetofts asks.

"In that! Ewwwwww!" Chloe says, pointing to a dollop of goat poo which Clover has left as a parting present.

"Play the music again!" Mrs Harris says. "Dancers, you'll have to go back on."

The villagers rush on again, carefully avoiding the poo patch. Mrs Lovetofts helps Chloe to her feet.

"Oww! I can't put any weight on it," Chloe says. "How am I going to walk on stage?"

"Someone will have to take over as queen," Mrs Harris says.

"But this is the best bit!" Chloe wails.

"Sorry, Chloe, but if you can't stand up . . . Emily, do you know the words?"

"Err . . . yes. I think so." All that time sitting in my rock box listening to the play means I could do any part.

"You'll have to do it. You'll have to be the queen," Mrs Harris says.

"Me?" I say, stunned.

"Yes, yes. You, Emily. I can't quite believe I'm saying it either, but the show must go on!"

I am in total shock-ness. I'm going to be the queen. Finally, after all these years, I'm going to say something other than "Quack."

Mrs Lovetofts helps Chloe up into a chair. "Here – put this on quickly," she says, handing me Chloe's robe. "It's got a few holes but it's all we've got."

As I sling the robe around my shoulders another thought occurs to me. If I'm going to be the queen in the final scene, Bella won't know I've lied. She will think it's been me all along in the black cloak. I'm saved! Thank you, Wavey Cat. You totally work in mysterious ways.

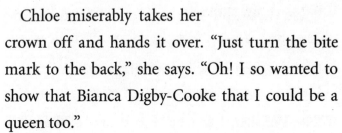

"And you need the crown," Mrs Lovetofts says.

Chloe miserably takes her crown off and hands it over. "Just turn the bite mark to the back," she says. "Oh! I so wanted to show that Bianca Digby-Cooke that I could be a queen too."

I put the crown on my head. It doesn't feel quite right. I move it about a bit but I know what the problem is. It's not meant for me. I look at Chloe, sitting there all fed up, and I think, *It's all wrong.* Chloe might be a pain, but she is really good at acting, and she did get everyone to work together and save the play from being a total disaster. And, if I'm totally honest, I'm not much good on the stage. I get table fright and mess up my lines and wave my arms about too much and knock things over. My special talents are camel whispering (although apparently not

249

goat whispering) and being creative. It's time to put some of that creativityness to good use.

"Here Chloe, put this back on." I hand her the crown. "You deserve to be queen."

"But she can't walk," Mrs Harris says. "What are you going to do – carry her?"

"No. Pull her. I just need to speak to Elaine," I say, running off down the stairs.

"Are you sure this is safe?" Chloe asks five minutes later, as the dancers stagger off stage, exhausted from their fourth country dance in a row.

"Just hold on to the edge," I say. Chloe sits on Elaine's tea trolley and grips on tightly. The gold tinsel Lena wrapped around it is doing a good job of making it look more royal. I've tied a rope to the handle for me to pull. (I borrowed it from Alfie

Balfour who was using it around the waist of his innkeeper's robe – I'm hoping this doesn't cause even more embarrassment later.) I've stuck the antlers on my head and I'm bravely wearing the second-hand red nose. With my grey T-shirt and leggings I make quite a passable reindeer.

"Finally, the spell was broken and the queen remembered who she was," Zuzanna says. The royal music plays. I stand in the wings, holding on to the rope, and stare out at the stage.

"Time to go on, Emily," Mrs Lovetofts whispers. I try to move my legs. They don't respond. The big empty stage looms ahead of me. The audience has gone quiet. I know everyone is waiting to see us but it is like the table fright all over again, or maybe this is trolley fright. Either way I can't move. My mouth is dry and my head feels a bit swimmy.

"Go," Mrs Harris says. "Hurry up, Emily."

From somewhere in the audience I hear a loud

squawk: "Ehhhhhhhhhh!" I know who that
is. Clover! Not goat Clover – baby Clover,
my little sister.

"Don't worry, Clover, We're coming!" I say. I
tug on the ropes and pull Chloe on to the stage
on her sparkly tea trolley coach. Her crown looks
magnificent and her golden robe flows out behind
her. I'm sure no one can really notice the holes
or the slight goat-poo stain on the bottom. The
audience laugh and clap. I pull Chloe right into the
middle of the stage and I turn and face everyone in
my red nose and antlers.

"Ehhhhhhhhhh!" cries Clover.

"The spell is broken!" Chloe says.
"Totally."

The audience laughs and claps
some more and the country dancers
stagger on one more time and we all
sing the last song to the sound of Mrs
Harris's clanking piano.

"Oh, the witch has cast a spell
The queen felt quite unwell
She forgot to wear a crown and robe
It's a very sad tale to tell.
But now the queen has found her memory
She really missed it terribly.
So have a good Christmas, everyone
Because soon it will be February!"

CHAPTER 18

How to Be a Mag Hall Girl

Friday night

When the curtain finally goes down, the audience are clapping so hard I can hardly hear the dancers gasping for breath.

"Well done, everyone – that was marvellous," Mrs Lovetofts says, helping Chloe down from her trolley-coach into a chair. "Emily, you saved the day!"

"Hmmph!" says Mrs Harris. "And now you can clean up this mess left by your goat friend." She hands me a cloth and bucket.

Elaine comes running up the stairs. "Well done, everybody! Now back to the dressing rooms. There will be a short break and then we will get everyone on stage to announce our Best Young Actor Award! Lena, you go too – the judges need to have a private chat."

For a minute I can't understand what she means. In all the excitement about goats and trollies and things I had totally forgotten about the award. Chloe limps off with Mrs Lovetofts to the First Aid room and the rest of us go downstairs.

"So," Bianca says when we get to our changing room. "How did it go, Juniper Road? Was your grand finale very grand?" She smiles. "There was certainly a lot of laughter."

"Well, there was a bit of an issue with a runaway goat," Zuzanna says, glaring at me.

"It was OK in the end, though," I say. "I pulled Chloe on stage on a tea trolley."

Bianca giggles. "I don't want to sound smug," she says, "but I do think we'll have to make room in the Mag Hall trophy cabinet again. It doesn't sound as if the Best Young Actor Award will be heading your way."

"We've had a lot of unexplained problems," Lena says. "I still don't understand how our scenery got damaged. Or how Chloe's costume ended up in the cleaning cupboard."

"In the cleaning cupboard? You were putting some things in the cleaning cupboard earlier, weren't you, Bianca?" Willow says. "Did you notice anything then?"

"You're talking too much again, Willow," Bianca says. "I keep telling you, we're not a chatty sort of school."

"What were you putting in there, anyway?" Willow continues. "It looked like an old curtain."

257

"It was Chloe's crown and robe, wasn't it?" Lena says.

Zuzanna gasps, "*You* put it in there?"

Bianca laughs. "Oh, all right. I confess," she says, throwing her hands up in the air. "It was no big deal, just a bit of fun."

"Like damaging our scenery and letting the goat out was a bit of fun, too?" Lena says.

Willow's eyes grow big and round. "You did that?" she says to Bianca.

"Look, Willow. What you need to understand is that Mag Hall is always the best. And if that means we have to sometimes succeed through, err ... alternative methods, well, that's just the way it is."

"But that's really mean! You messed up their play on purpose," Willow says.

"You are *so* not a Mag Hall girl," Bianca snaps. "Just like Chloe Clarke – and we all know what sort of girl she was."

"I thought she was quite nice," says a quiet voice.

"What?"

"I said, I thought she was quite nice. I liked Chloe, she was fun," Naemah says more loudly. "Until you started picking on her."

"I don't know what you mean," Bianca says. "I never pick on anyone."

"Actually, you do," Edwina sniffs. "You pick on everyone, Bianca. You made me get your PE bag from the field in the pouring rain last week and now I've got a cold."

"And you picked on Chloe so much that she left school," Naemah adds. "Just because she got the lead role in the school play."

"What?" Bianca says. "That's so not true. Tell them, Lavender."

Lavender looks uncomfortable and chews the end of her plait.

"It is true," Edwina sniffs. "We should have stuck up for her ... but we didn't."

"But you said Chloe was excluded," Zuzanna says.

"I never said she was excluded," Bianca says. "I said she had to leave. Which she did – her mother made her."

"Because her mother was so worried about her being bullied, she took her out of school," Naemah says.

"So Chloe wasn't bullying anyone?" I say. "You made it up."

"I've had quite enough of listening to all this," Bianca says, standing up.

There's a knock at the door and Elaine pops her head round. "Ready for the results, girls? You're all wanted up on stage."

"Come on, girls," Bianca says. "Time for me to collect my award." She walks towards the door, but the others look a bit uncertain about whether to follow her.

"Come on," she snaps. "Willow, hurry up."

"I'm not sure I want to go with you, any more," Willow says.

"You go ahead and get your award, Bianca," Naemah says. "Willow can come with me."

"And me," Edwina sniffs.

"What? Lavender, are you coming? Surely you're not going to side with them, too?" Bianca says.

Lavender spits out her plait and says, "Do you know what, Bianca? I don't really think you're a Mag Hall sort of girl."

"You so don't deserve me as a friend! Any of you. I'm going where I'm appreciated!" Bianca says and slams out of the room.

"Sorry about that, Juniper Road," Lavender says. "I hope you realise we're not all like Bianca. Still, I suppose we'd better get up on stage."

"Yes, we'd better go," Naemah says. "It's for Mag Hall, remember?" and they burst into giggles and walk out.

"But I don't understand," Zuzanna says, looking utterly confused. "I thought Bianca was nice."

"I've met a lot of girls like her," Lena says. "They are all nice on the outside and not at all nice underneath."

"But how did you know she damaged the scenery and let the goat out?" I ask.

"I didn't," Lena says. "Just call it a pretty good guess."

"But ... I was really mean to Chloe," Zuzanna says. "I need to say sorry."

"We've got to go on stage first," I say. "Come on, they'll be waiting.

CHAPTER 19

All's Well That Ends Well

Friday night

"Now," Elaine says, when we are all gathered at the side of the stage. "I will go out and introduce you. Then you all come on to the stage, hopefully to a nice round of applause, and then we will present the Best Young Actor Award."

Elaine walks on to the stage and disappears through the curtains to address the audience.

"Ladies and Gentlemen."

The audience quietens down.

"Thank you so much for coming. I'm sure you want to join with me in thanking all the young actors we've seen tonight for entertaining us so beautifully." The audience burst into applause again and I feel my legs go all wobbly. Really, they have a life of their own. "The judges were very impressed with the Juniper Road performances," Elaine continues. "Some of their play was described as 'comedy gold'. Especially the runaway goat."

"Ehhhhhhhhhhhh!" says my baby sister. There are giggles from the audience.

"Well, even that was down to me, really," Bianca says, then bites her lip.

"And of course, a wonderful performance from all the Magnolia Hall girls. So if I could ask both schools to come on to the stage for one last time I'm sure you'll join me in showing your appreciation."

There is a huge round of applause.

"Excuse me," Bianca says, pushing past me, "I have an award to collect."

The Mag Hall girls file on to the stage, followed by Mr Garrick with a smug look on his face. All the littlees rush on too and sit at the front looking like tiny angels.

Mrs Lovetofts and Mrs Harris help Chloe limp on to the stage and we all follow on behind.

We take a bow (Chloe sort of takes a dip) and everyone claps and cheers again.

"And now," Elaine says, "time to announce this year's Shoestring Theatre Best Young Actor Award. And this year the award goes to ... Amy-Lee Langer for her highly convincing portrayal of a witch!"

"What?" Bianca cries. "What about me? I'm the queen!" There is a sort of hush as everyone looks at Bianca. "But I am! Everyone knows I'm the best actor. I always am!" There are a few giggles from the audience. Bianca sucks in her cheeks and says "Urrhhh!" and storms off the stage.

Elaine clears her throat. "Ahem. Well, as I said, congratulations, Amy-Lee!"

"Yeah!" Yeah-Yeah Yasmin says.

There is a huge round of applause. Amy-Lee goes very pink. Elaine hands her a gold-coloured plastic cup and Amy-Lee looks at it as if it's something that doesn't belong to her. Mrs Lovetofts walks her to the front of the stage and makes her do a lot of bowing.

Finally the curtains close and we get to leave the stage. Zuzanna and I help Chloe down the steps. Bianca comes out of the dressing room towards us and hurries quickly past. She has already changed and got her bag and definitely doesn't seem to be in the mood for talking.

"I need to say sorry," Zuzanna says after we've helped Chloe into a chair. "I made a big mistake about Bianca. You were right – she's not very nice at all."

"I'm usually right, Zuzanna, you should know that by now," Chloe says.

"She told us you were bullying the little kids," I say.

"And you believed her?" Chloe says, looking straight at me and making me feel uncomfortable.

"Well, maybe, no, I ... Why didn't you tell us about what happened at Mag Hall?" I say.

"I don't know. Because I wanted to forget all about it," Chloe says, "and I didn't want you to think I was, well the sort of person who gets bullied."

"I don't think there is a sort of person," I say. "It happened to you and Lena and you're not the same at all."

"True," Chloe says. "I suppose not all schools are as nice as Juniper Road."

"Wow, that's the first time you've said that," I say.

"Yes," Chloe says thoughtfully. "Although the school I was at before Mag Hall was brilliant. Did I ever tell you about it? It's called Upton Abbey and it had its own film studio and stables and a swimming pool with water-slides—"

"I need to find Bella," I say. "I'll see you later."

The foyer is really crowded. All the mums and dads are shaking hands and chatting and Amy-Lee is walking around with her award like she's at an Oscar Ceremony. Naemah and Willow are standing together, laughing. Bianca has apparently already gone home with her parents.

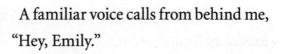A familiar voice calls from behind me, "Hey, Emily."

"Oh. Hi, Bella," I say, and then I don't know what else to say so I sort of give her an awkward smile.

"So you weren't the queen then?" She sounds disappointed.

"No, I didn't feel well and then I felt better and then I had to swap parts and . . . "

Bella is looking at me like I'm speaking a foreign language.

I sigh. "OK. I'm sorry. I sort of made it up. I was never the queen. Mostly, I was a rock."

"I thought I recognised those feet." She smiles a little. "But why didn't you tell me?"

"Because I wanted you to think I had a good part for once. Because New Emily is a good actor and I'm just rubbish."

"But you're good at loads of things that New Emily's not."

"Like what? Messing things up?"

"Yes, you're good at that." She grins. "But you're also good at poems and making stuff and being funny. And worrying. You're an excellent worrier!"

"I'm really sorry. You only came to the play because you thought I was the star."

"You were! Rudolph really made the play – pulling that tea trolley on at the end was hilarious. I can't wait to tell New Emily all about it."

"Oh, dear. Or do I mean *oh, deer*," I say, waggling my hands on my head like antlers.

"See? You're funny. I can't wait to tell her how my best friend Emily was a star performer ... Of course, you weren't as good as Clover." And we laugh so much that Bella's mum comes over to make sure we're OK.

"Sorry, girls. We've got to go – it's a long drive back to Wales in the morning," she says.

"It was really good to see you," I say, giving Bella a hug.

"You too. Next time, you need to come to Wales."

"Really?"

"Yes. Definitely. I want New Emily to meet ... Emily the First! See, you should have been queen!"

I am definitely adding that to my ruler ruler when I get home.

ACKNOWLEDGEMENTS

Living with someone when they're trying to write a book is a very difficult thing. Writers swing from overexcitement to irritability for no discernible reason, and frequently shut themselves in cupboards "to think". Therefore I would like to thank my incredibly patient family, for remaining calm and composed throughout, despite my ravings, and for always rallying to the cry of "More tea!"

Thank you also to my lovely mum, who has now found a second career as a copy-editor and could debate the finer points of the subjunctive with an Oxford don.

Special thanks to brilliant book blogger Jim (@YAYeahYeah) for always being Emily's number one fan and supporter.

A million thanks as ever to the super-fantastic Little, Brown Books for Young Readers team, especially my wonderful editor Kate Agar, who always helps me find the wood through the trees and without whom this book would be around three times the length and mostly about Finnish herrings.

And finally, thanks to Gemma Cooper – for enthusiasm, encouragement and always keeping the faith, but mostly for just for being Gemma. Everyone should have one.

ABOUT THE AUTHOR

Ruth Fitzgerald was born in Bridgend, South Wales. She grew up in a happy, big noisy family with far too many brothers.

When she was six years old she wrote her first story, "Mitzi the Mole Gets Married", and *immediately* announced she wanted to be a writer. Her teacher *immediately* advised her that writing was a hobby and she needed to get a proper job. Since then she has tried twenty-three proper jobs but really the only thing she likes doing is writing.

Ruth lives in Suffolk with her family, one very small dog and five chickens. They are all very supportive of her writing, although the chickens don't say a lot.

Have you read all the fab Emily Sparkes books?

For Emily Sparkes news, reviews
and totally awesome downloads
visit www.ruthfitzgerald.co.uk